HELLO KITTY®
Work of Art

stories and art by
Giovanni Castro, Jacob Chabot, Ian McGinty and Jorge Monlongo

hello kitty shorts by
Maite Oz

HELLO KITTY

Work of Art

Cover Art Jacob Chabot
Cover and Book Design Shawn Carrico
Editor Traci N. Todd

Printed in China

Published by VIZ Media, LLC
P.O. Box 77010
San Francisco, CA 94107

10 9 8 7 6 5 4 3 2 1
First printing, November 2014

"The Doodles," "Weld Done," "Mustache Mystery in the Art Museum,"
"Pottery Pandemonium" and "Say Cheese"
Stories and art by Ian McGinty, colors by Fred C. Stresing

"Surprise Performace," "Natural Talent" and "An Unexpected Journey"
Stories and art by Giovanni Castro

"Paintings"
Story and art by Jorge Monlongo

"Watercolor," "Music Dreams" and "Sweet Project"
Stories and art by Maite Oz

RATED A FOR ALL AGES
PARENTAL ADVISORY
HELLO KITTY: WORK OF ART is rated A and is suitable for readers of all ages.
ratings.viz.com

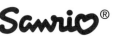

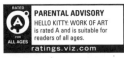

Contents

Family

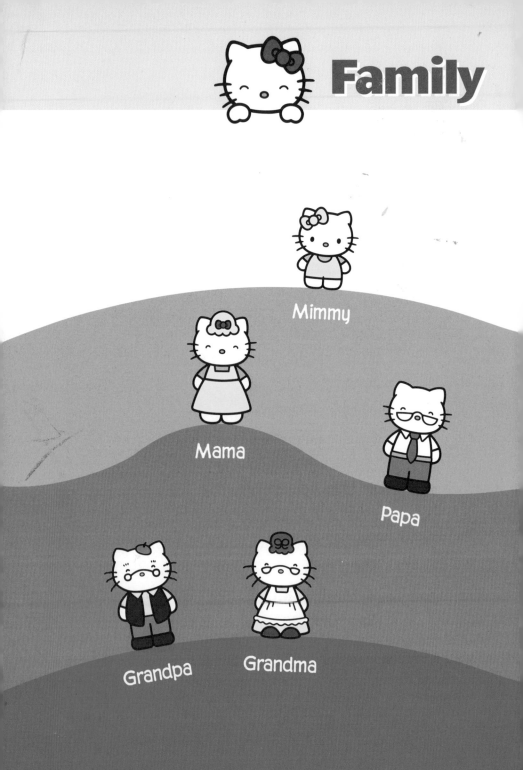

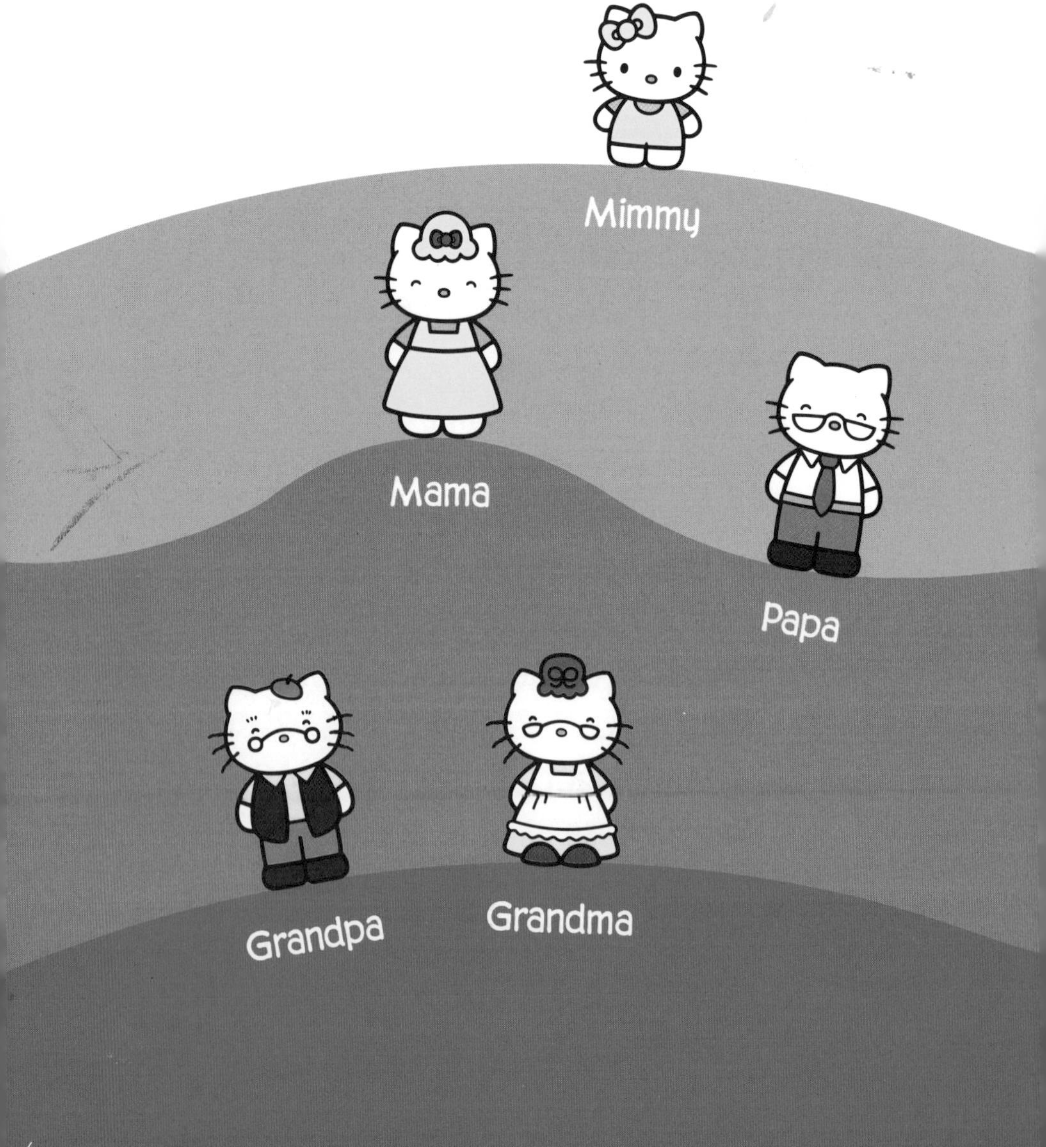
Mimmy
Mama
Papa
Grandpa
Grandma

and Friends

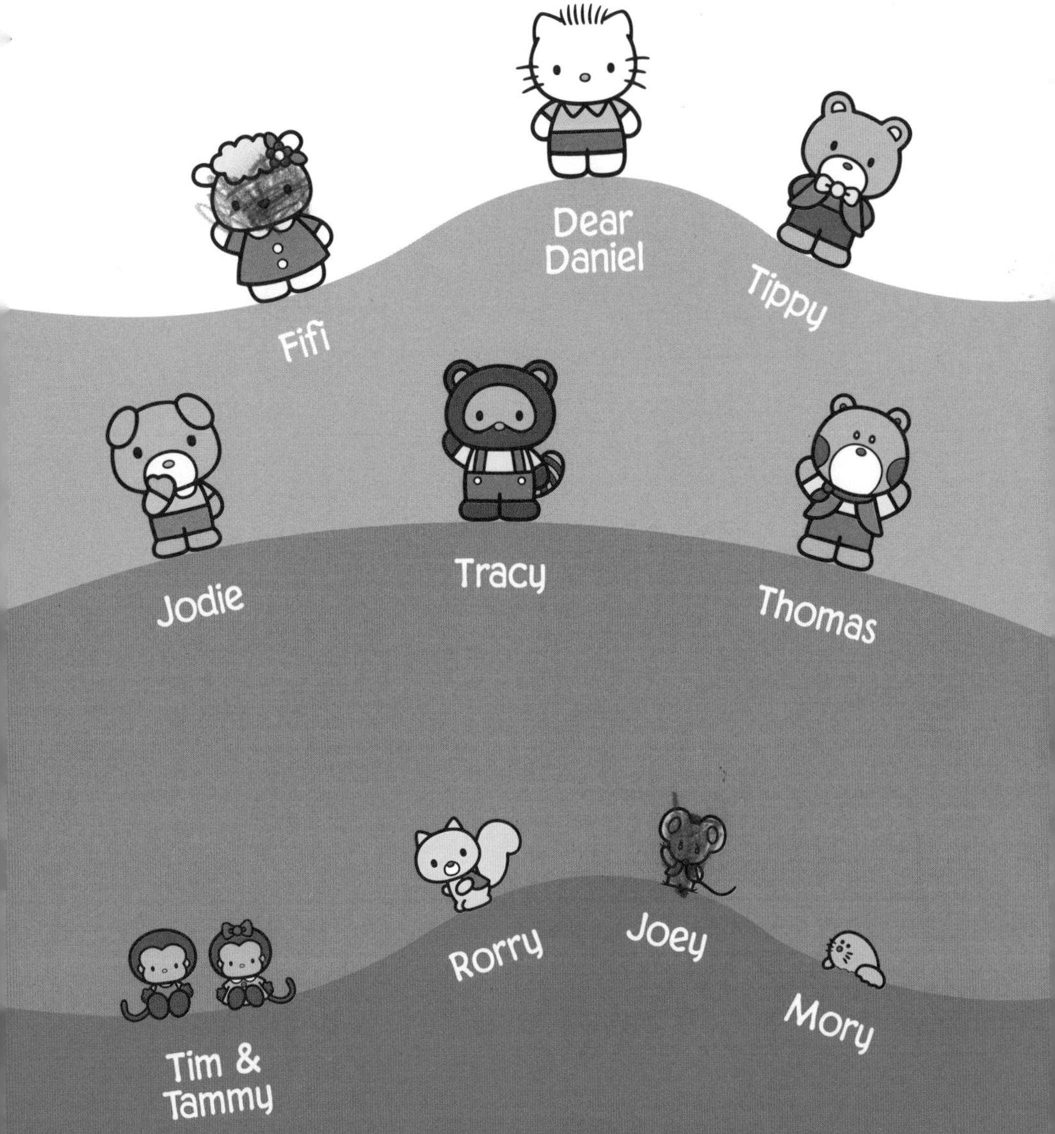
Dear Daniel
Fifi
Tippy
Jodie
Tracy
Thomas
Rorry
Joey
Mory
Tim & Tammy

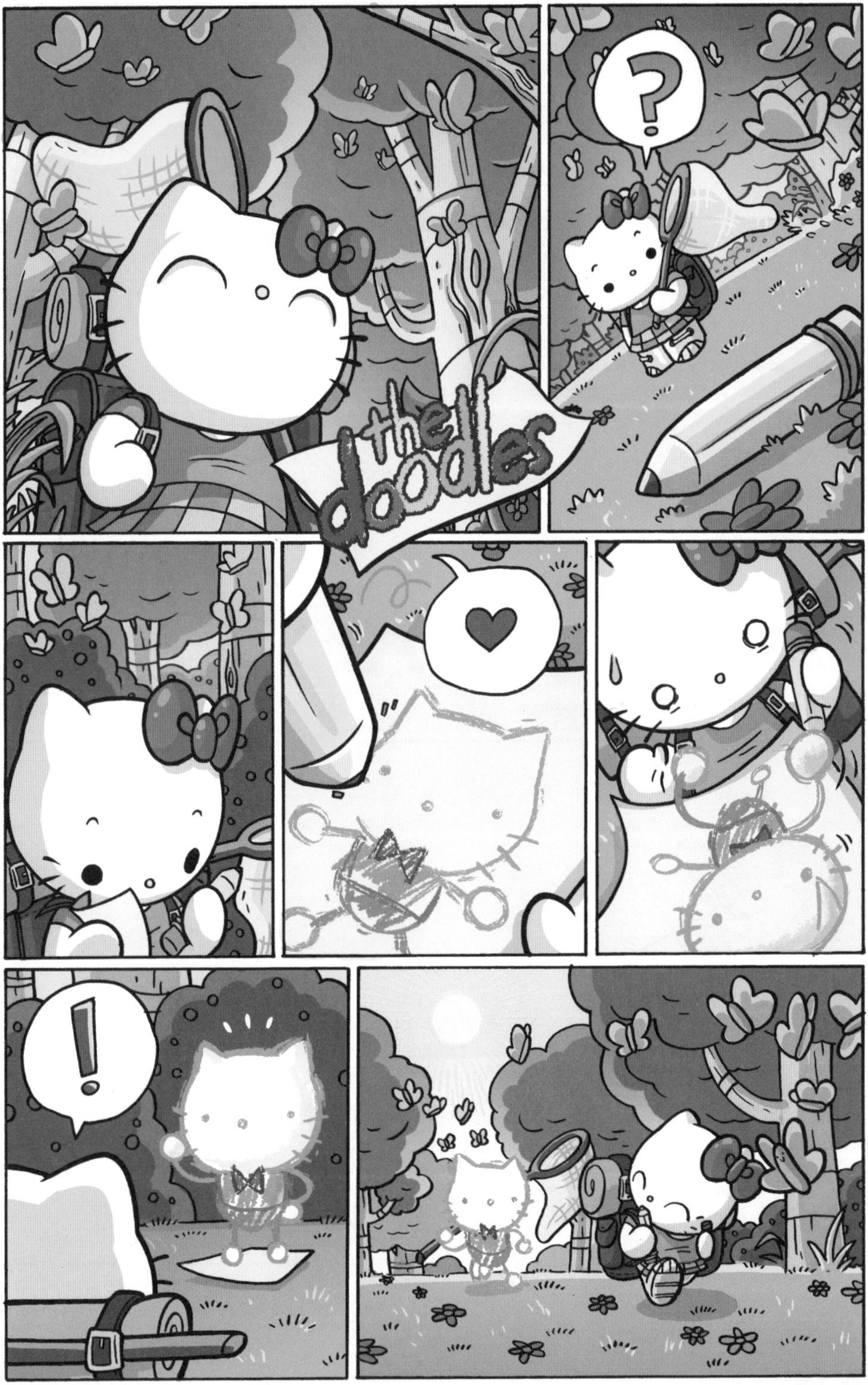
the doodles
?
!

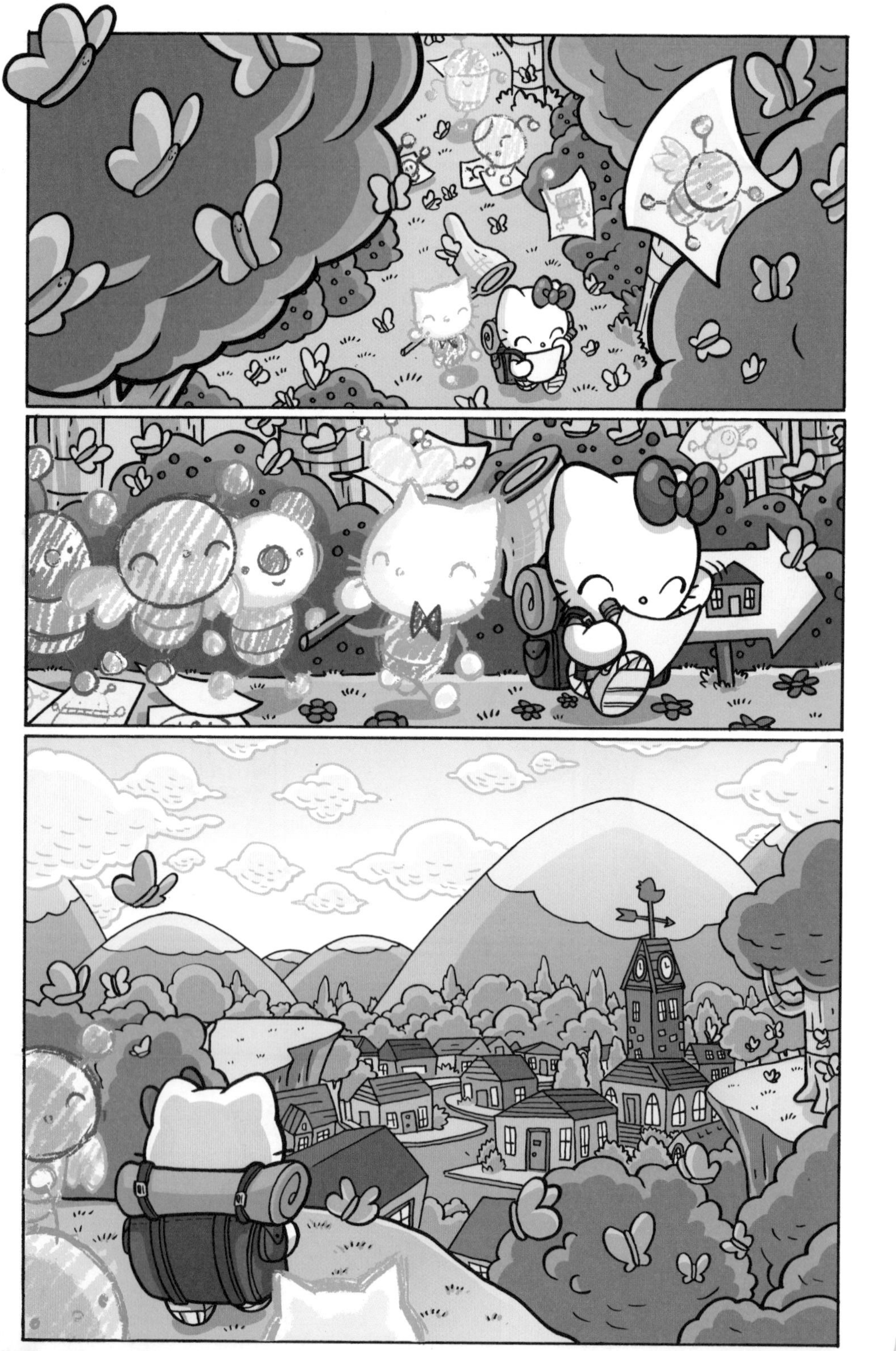

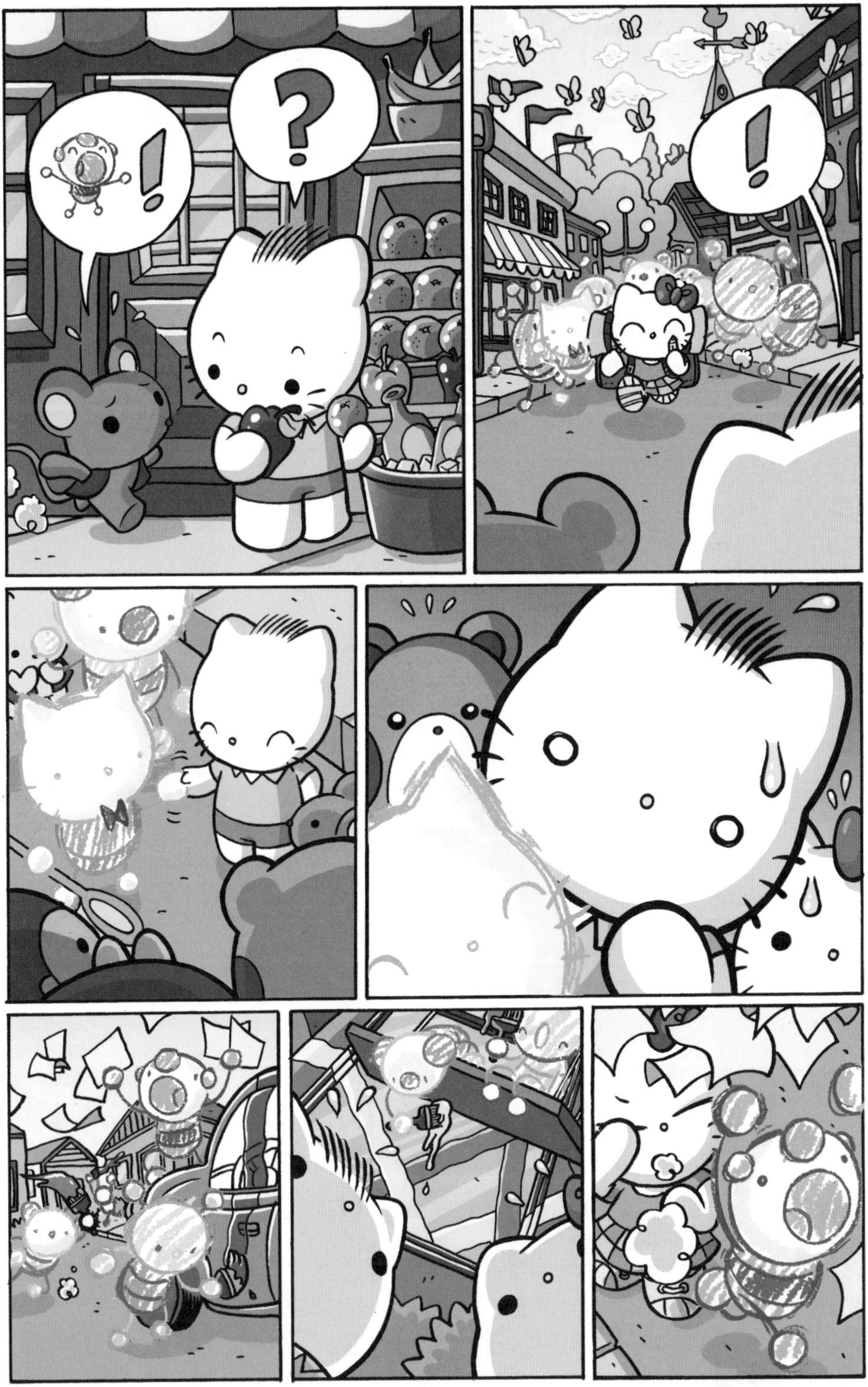
!
?
!

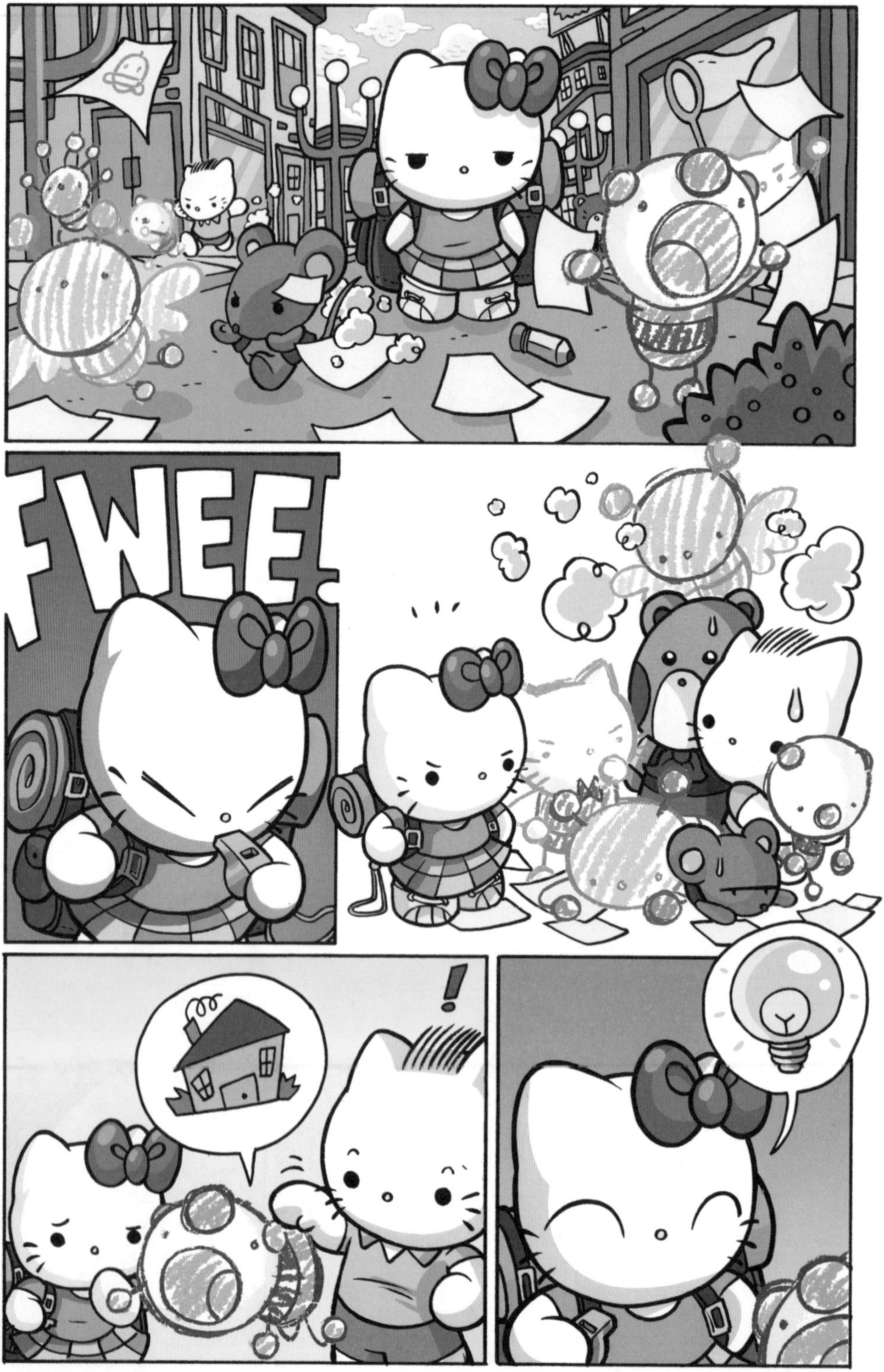
FWEE
!

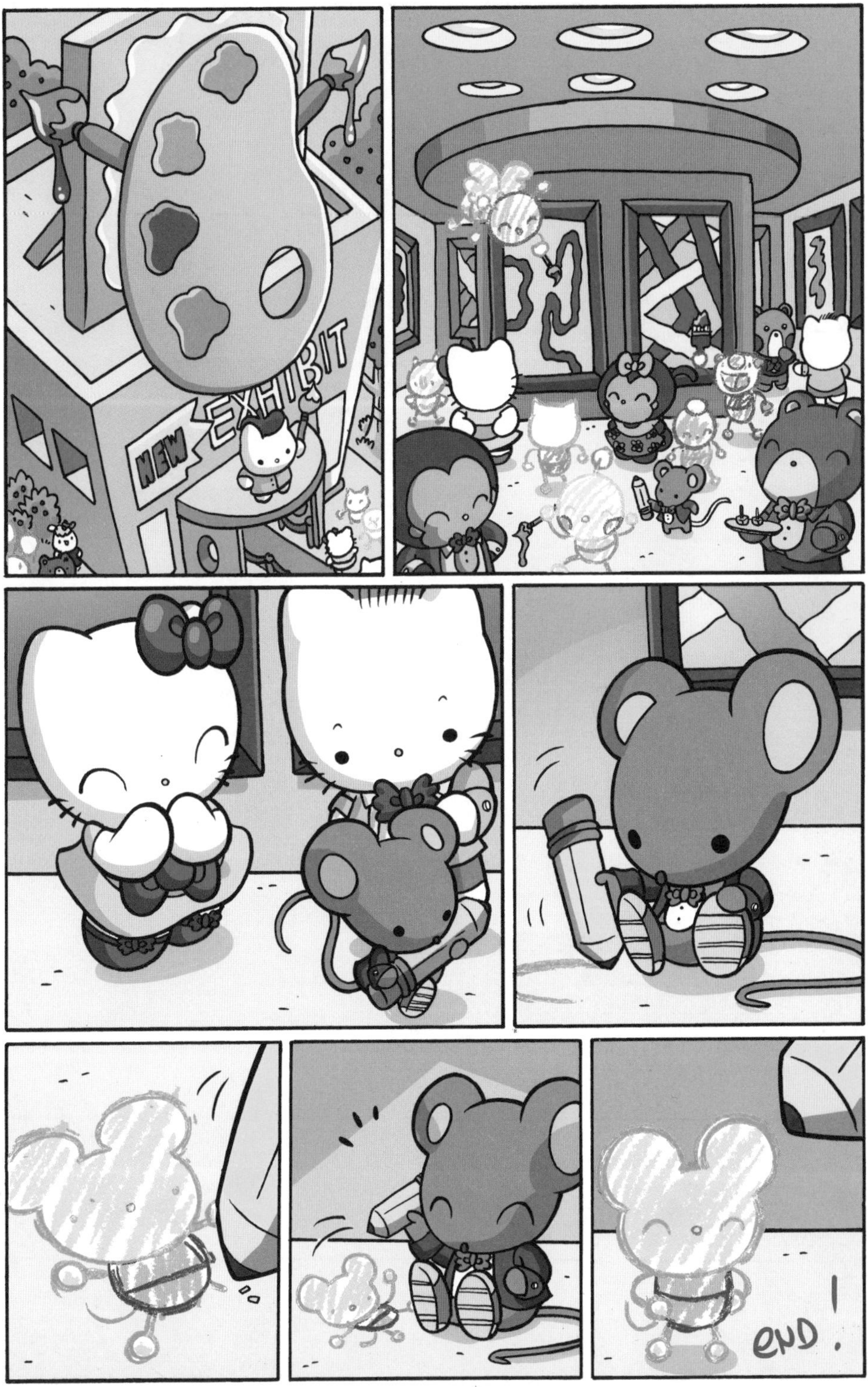
NEW EXHIBIT
END!

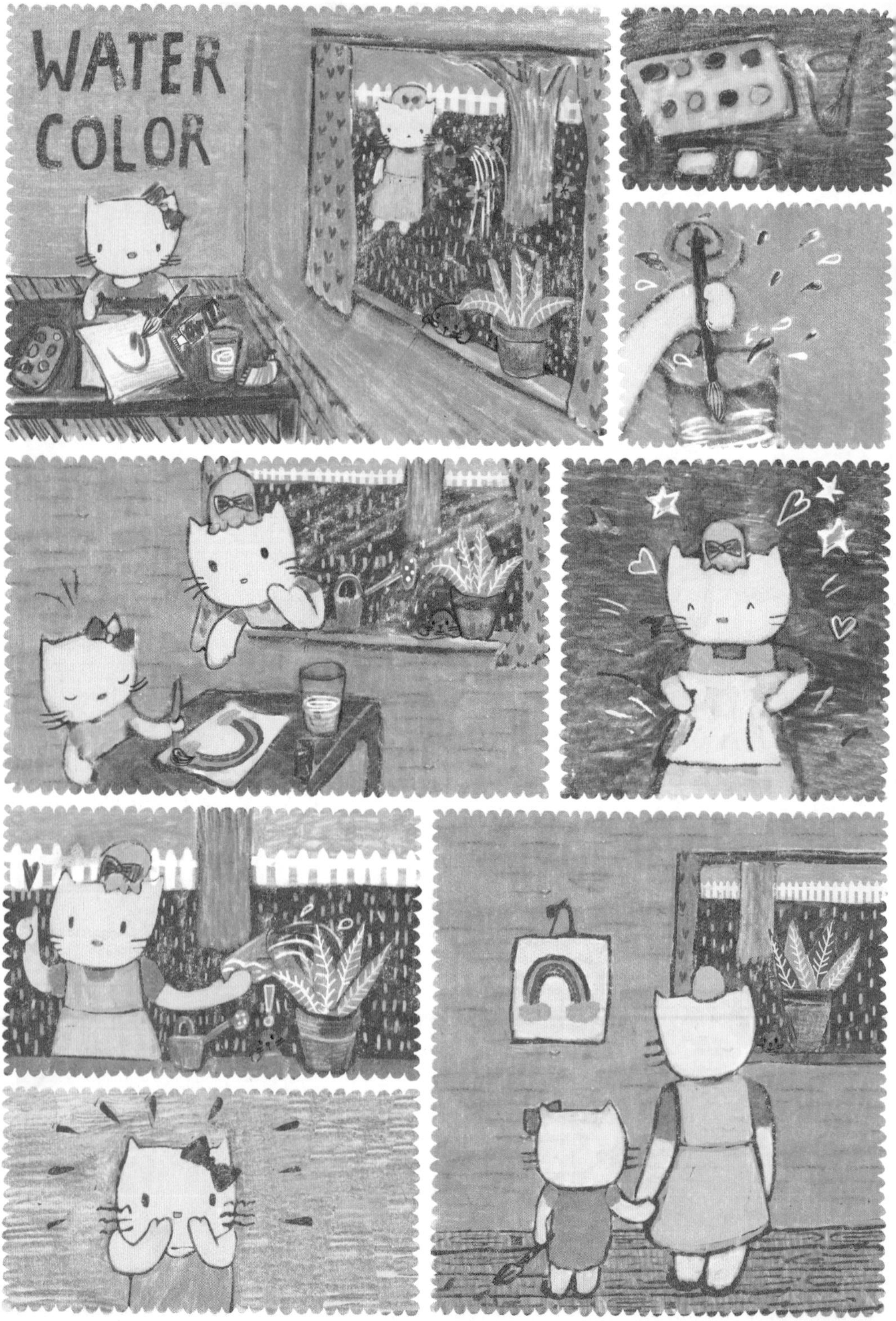
WATER
COLOR

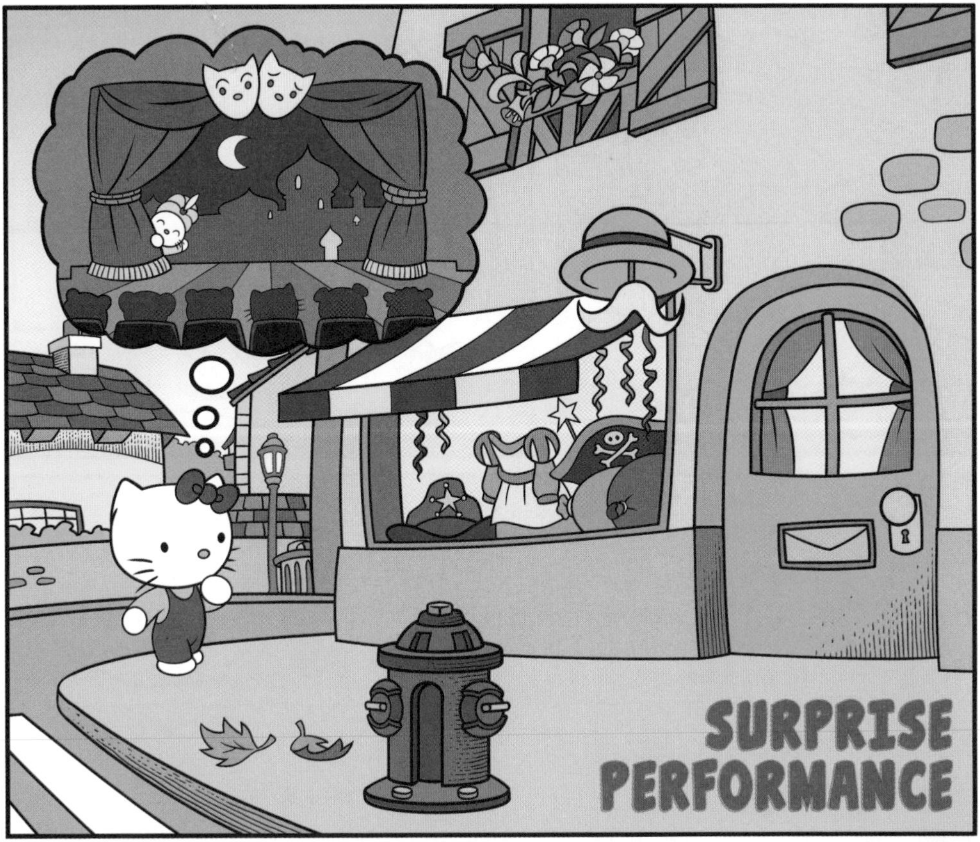
SURPRISE
PERFORMANCE

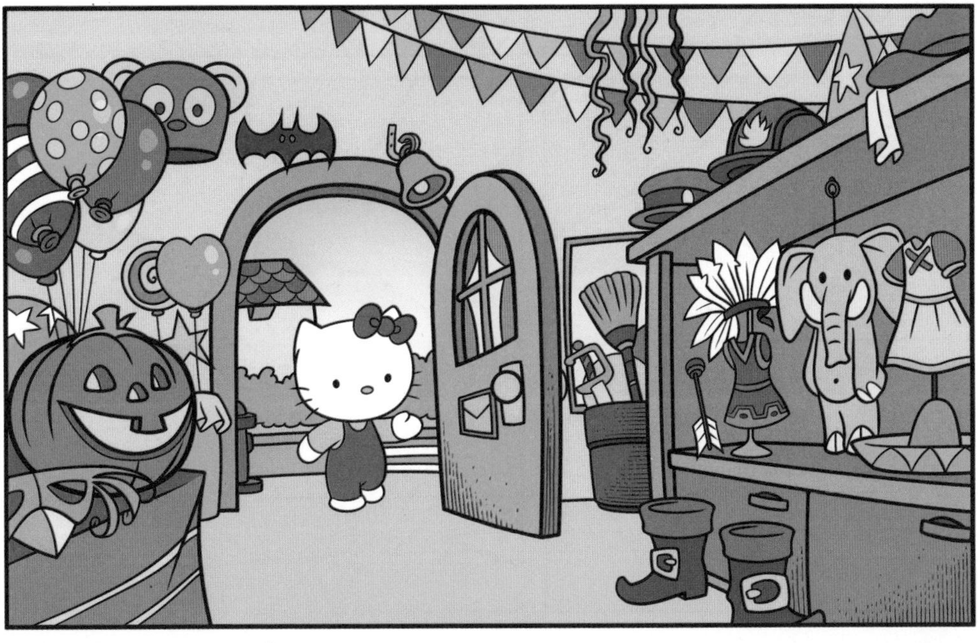

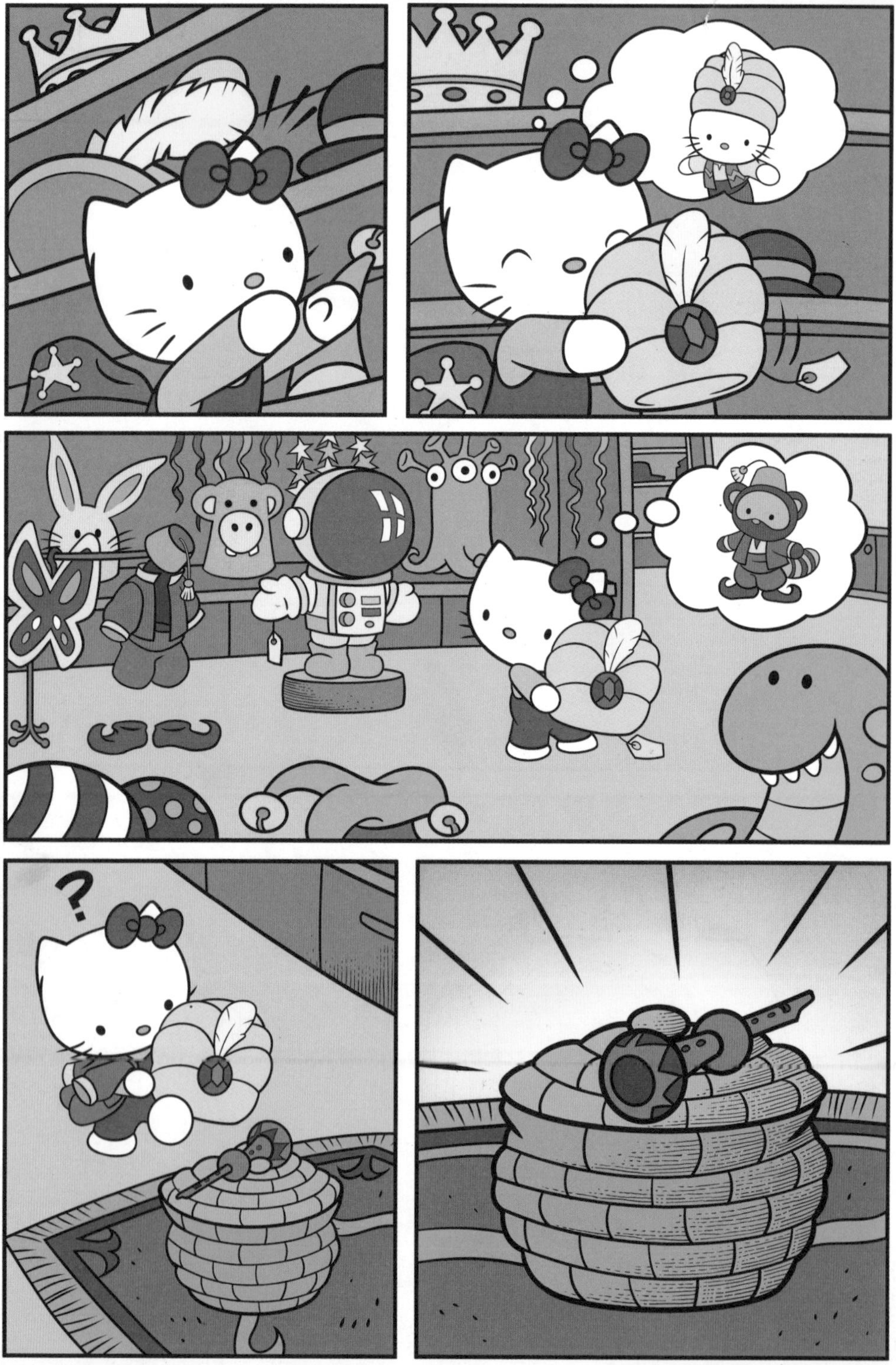
?

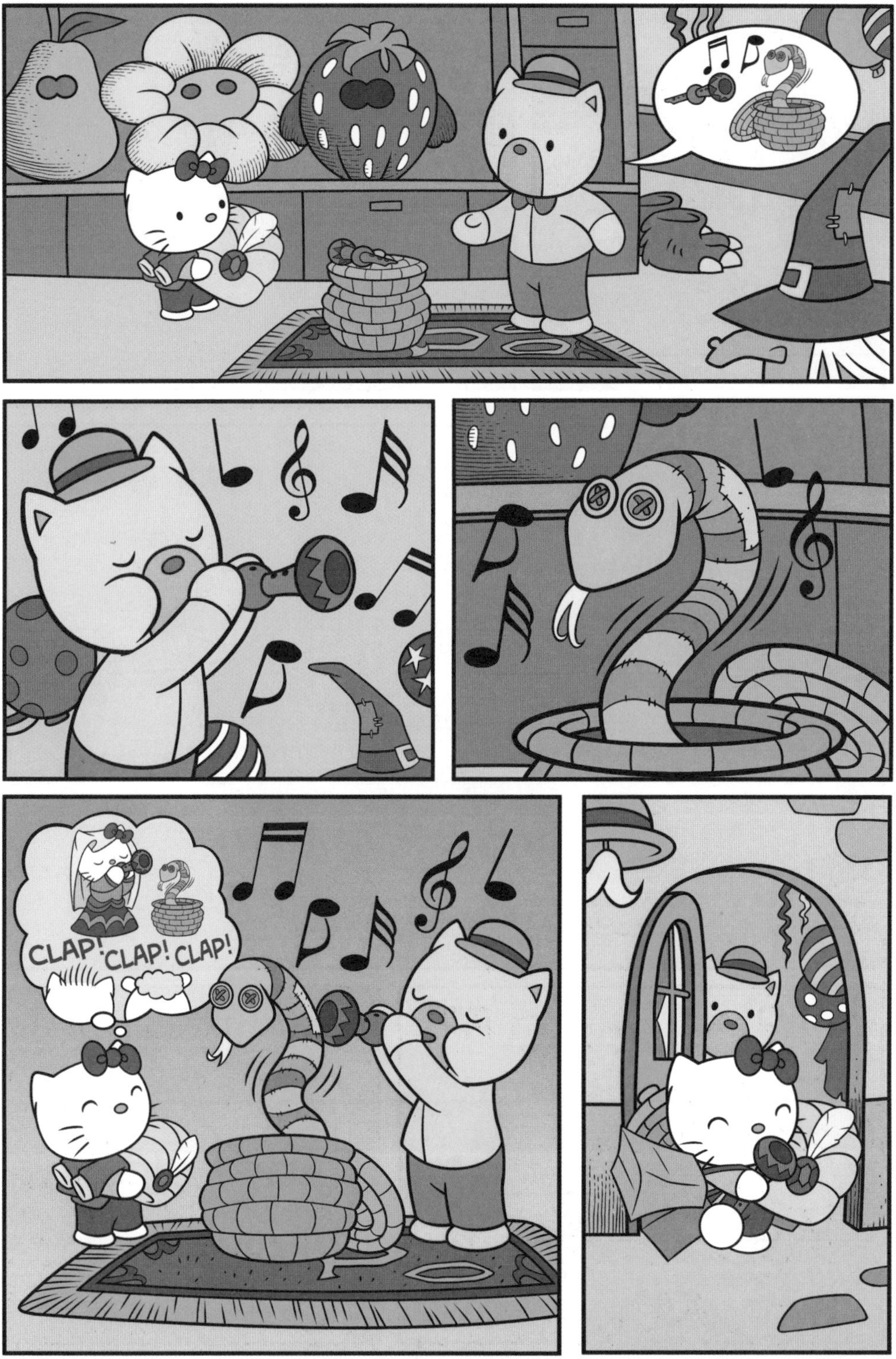
CLAP! CLAP! CLAP!

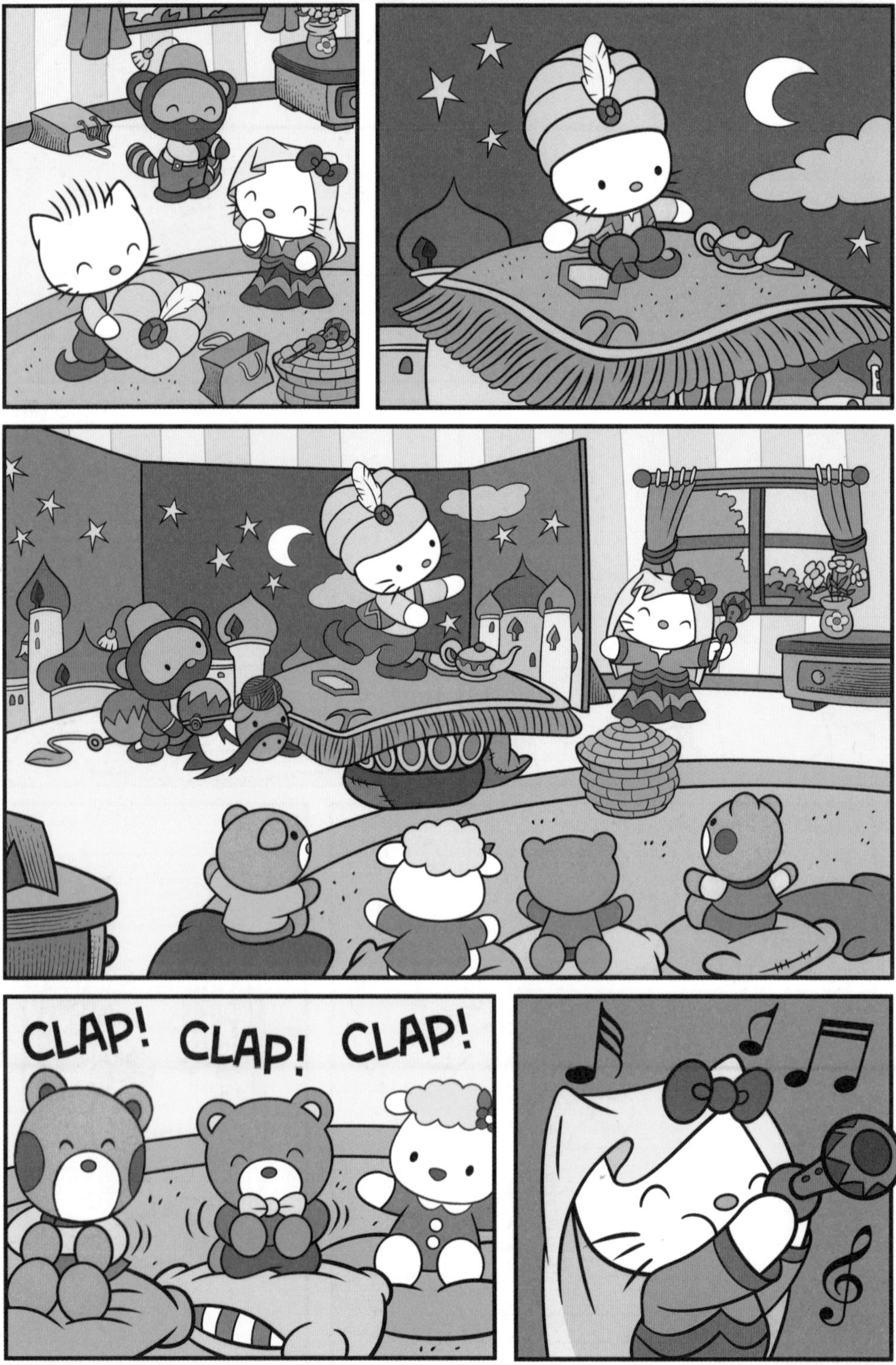
CLAP! CLAP! CLAP!

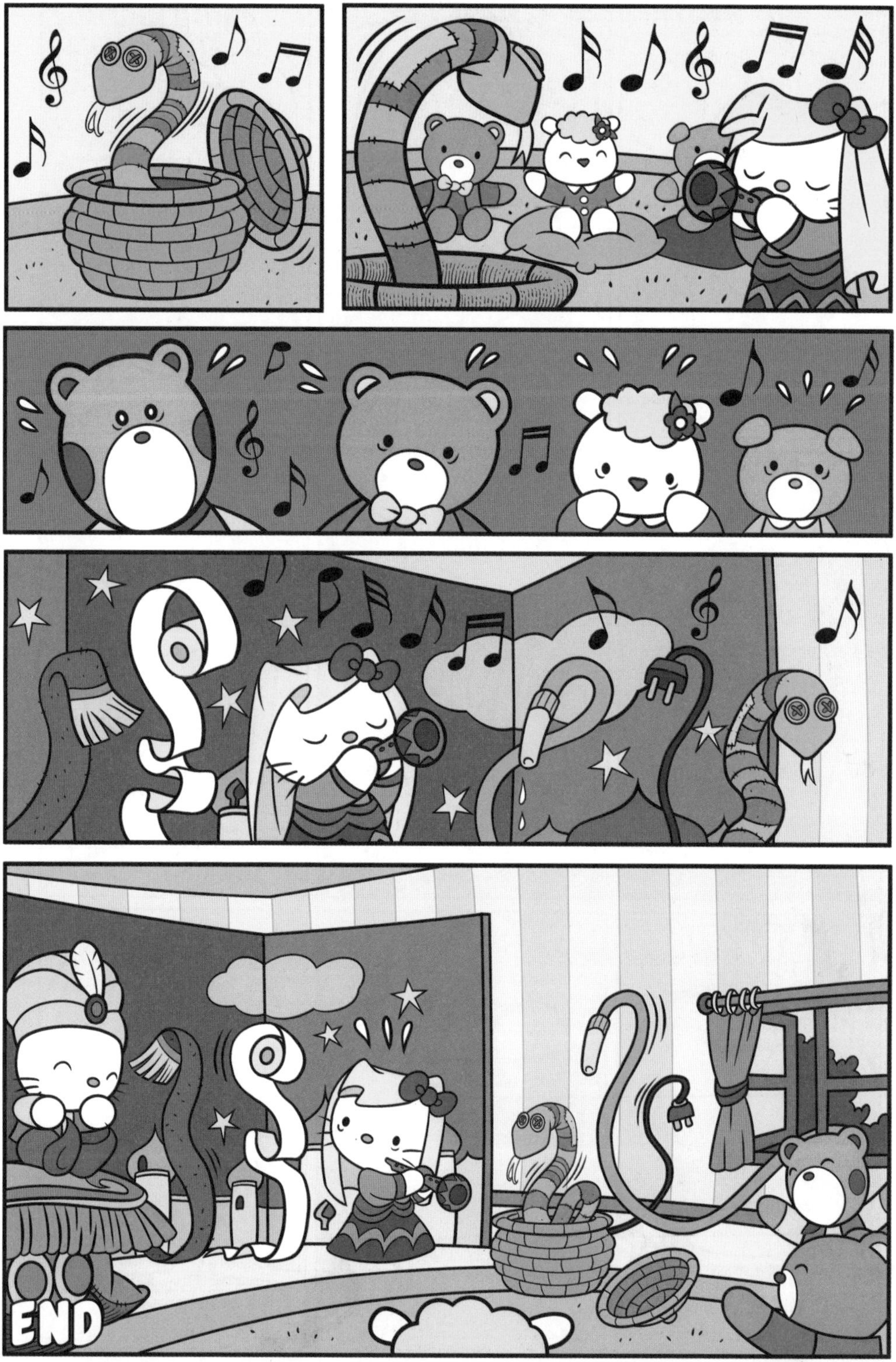
END

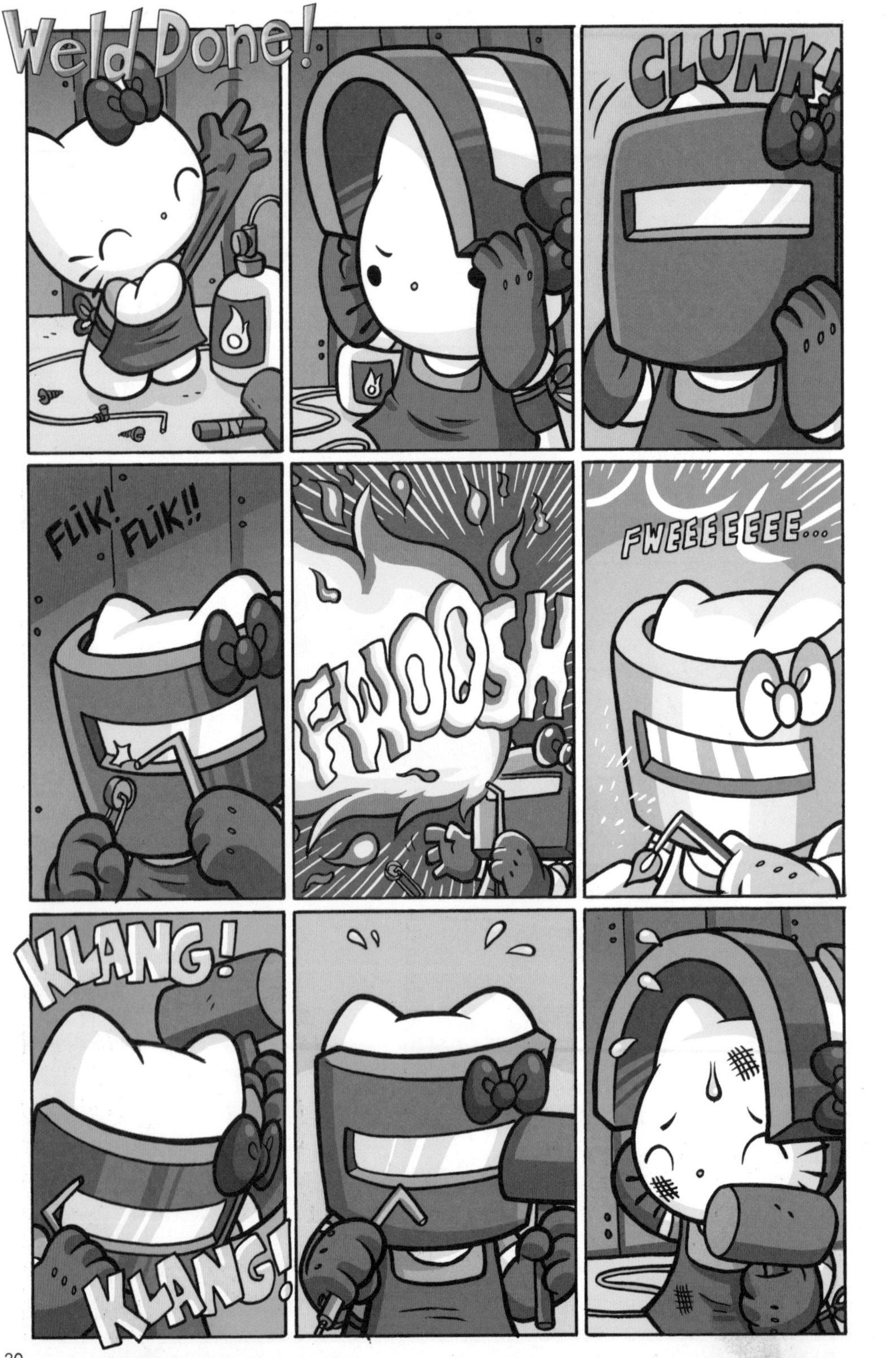
Weld Done!
CLUNK!
FLIK! FLIK!!
FWOOSH
FWEEEEEEE...
KLANG!
KLANG!

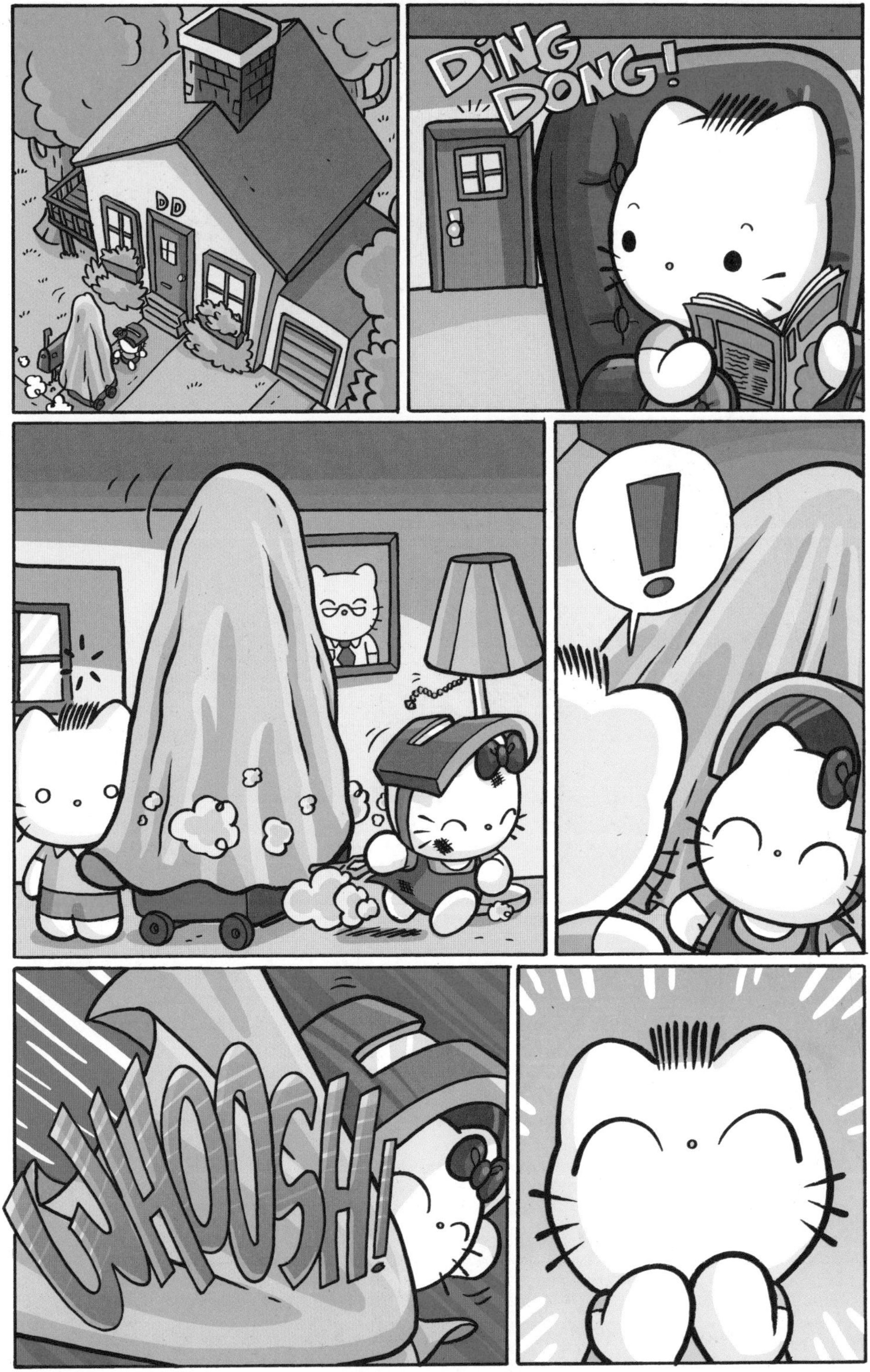
DD
DING DONG!
!
WHOOSH!

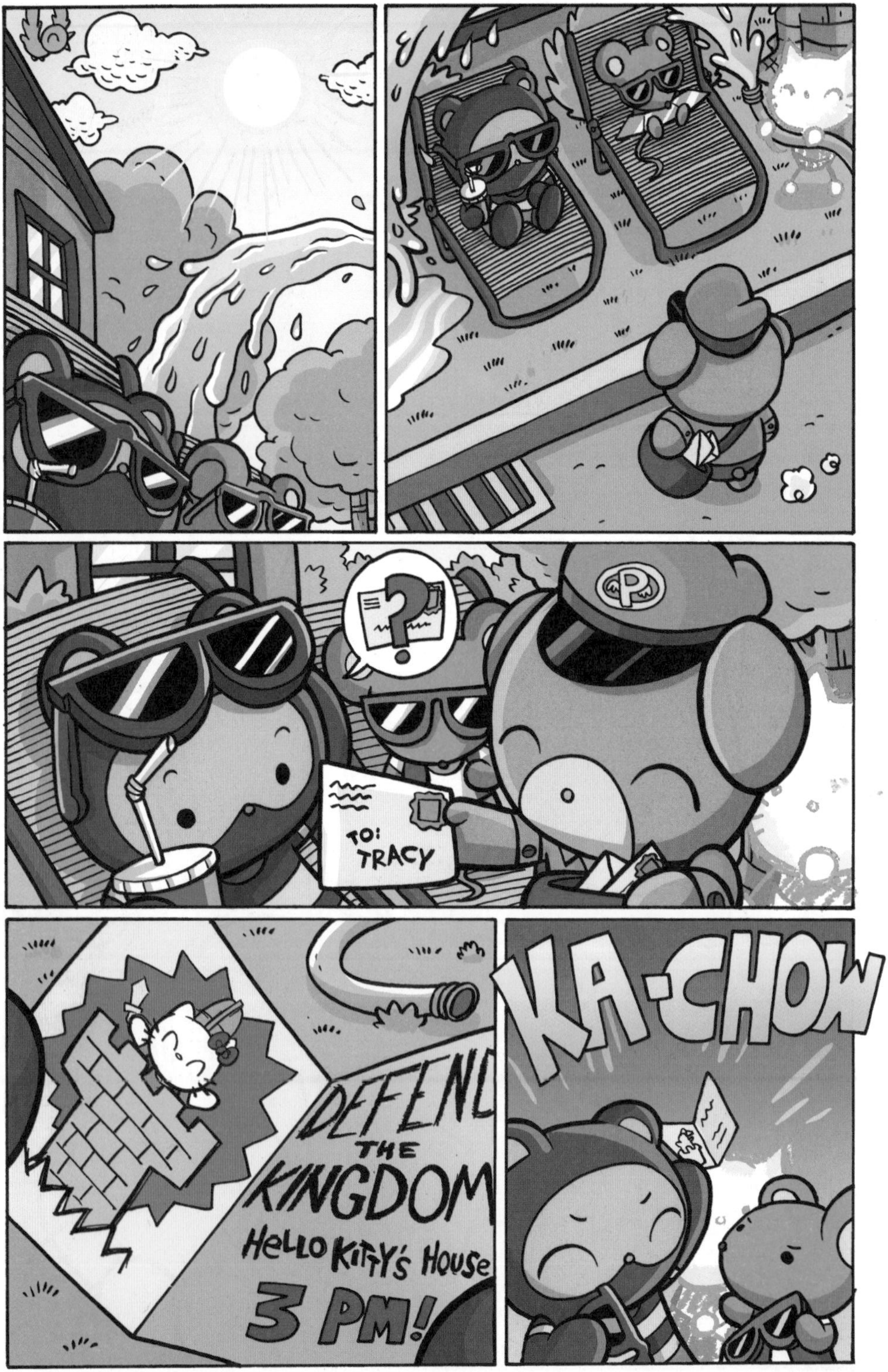
TO: TRACY
DEFEND THE KINGDOM
HELLO KITTY'S HOUSE
3 PM!
KA-CHOW

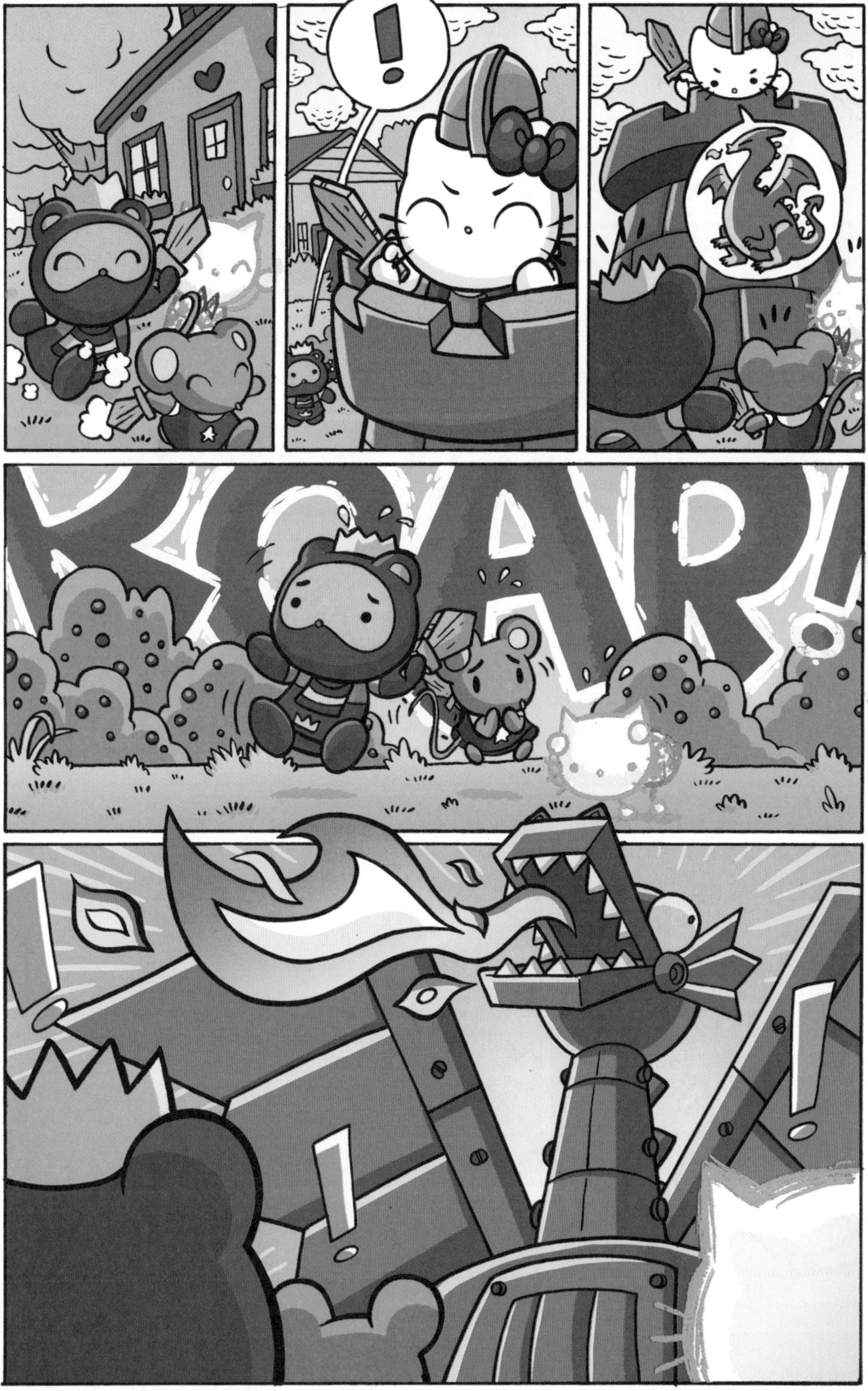
!
ROAR!

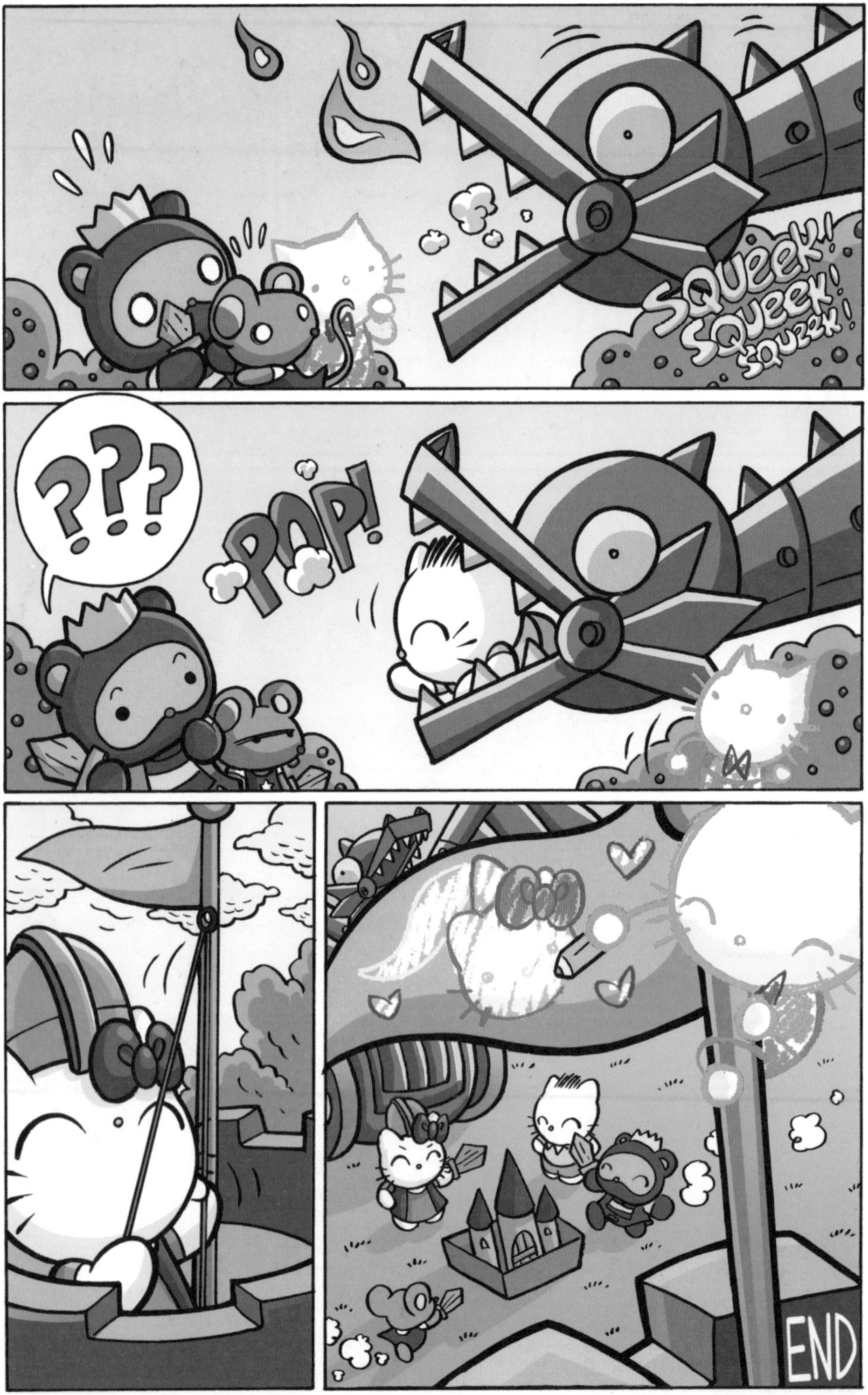
SQUEEK! SQUEEK! SQUEEK!
???
POP!
END

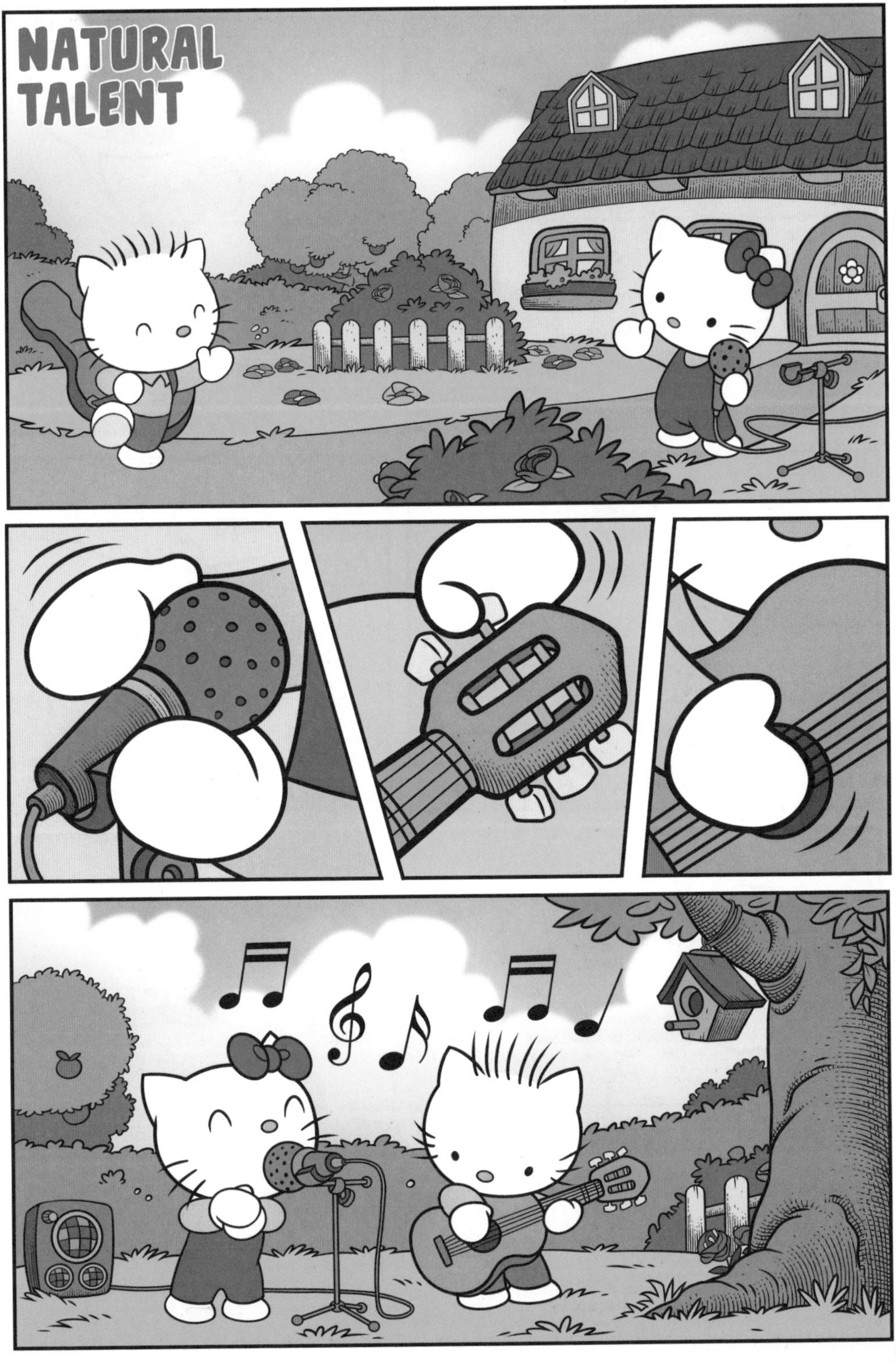
NATURAL TALENT

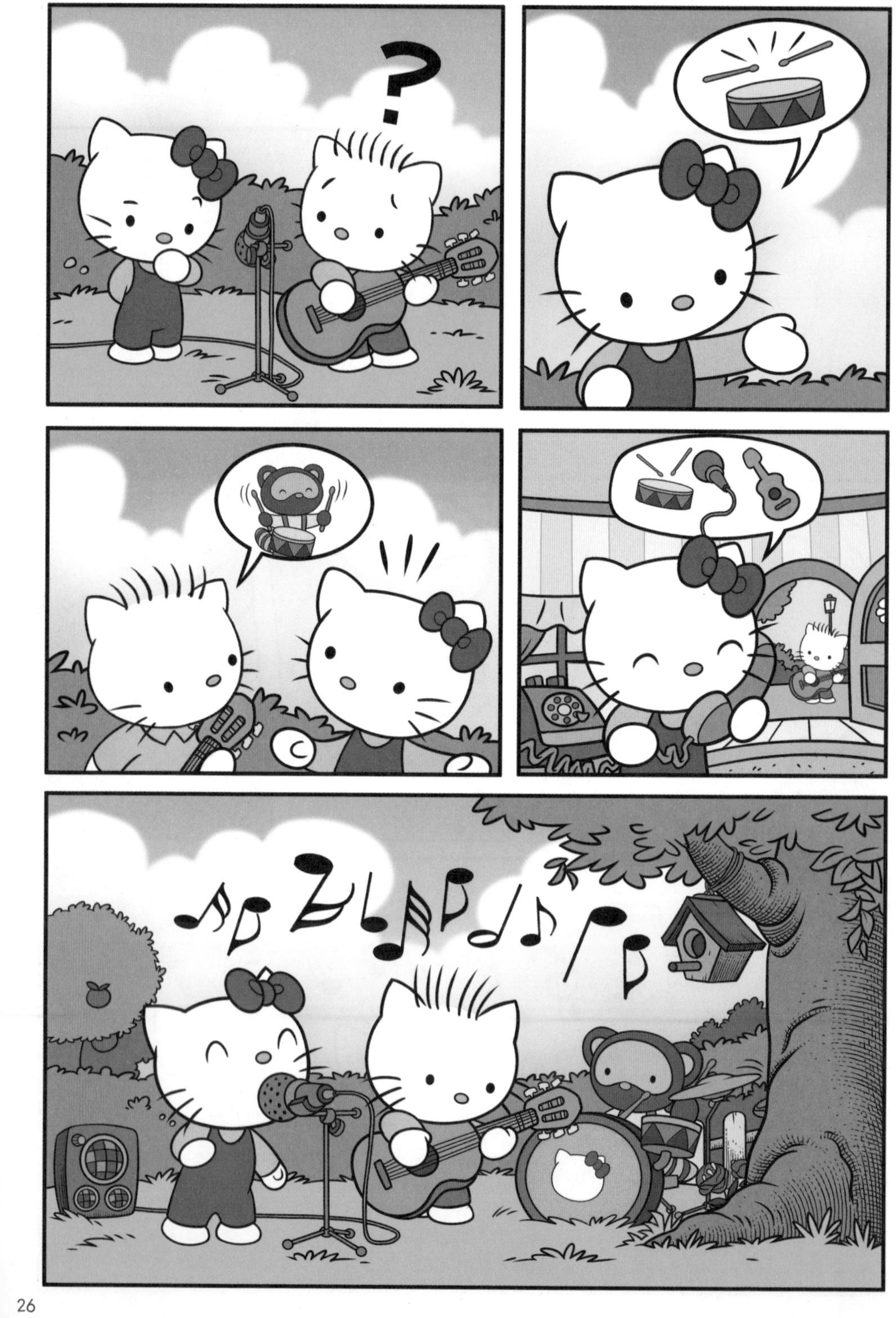
?

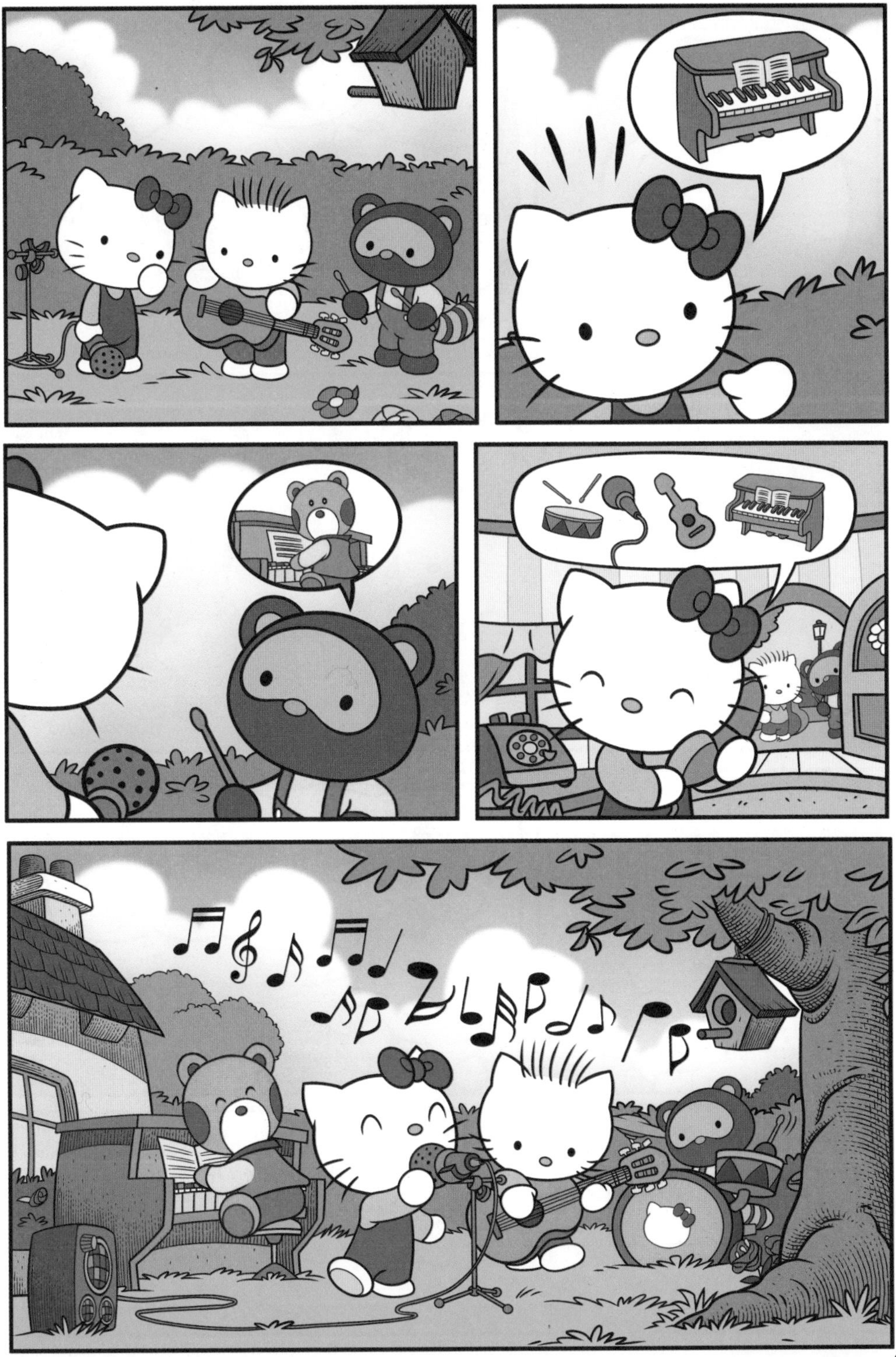

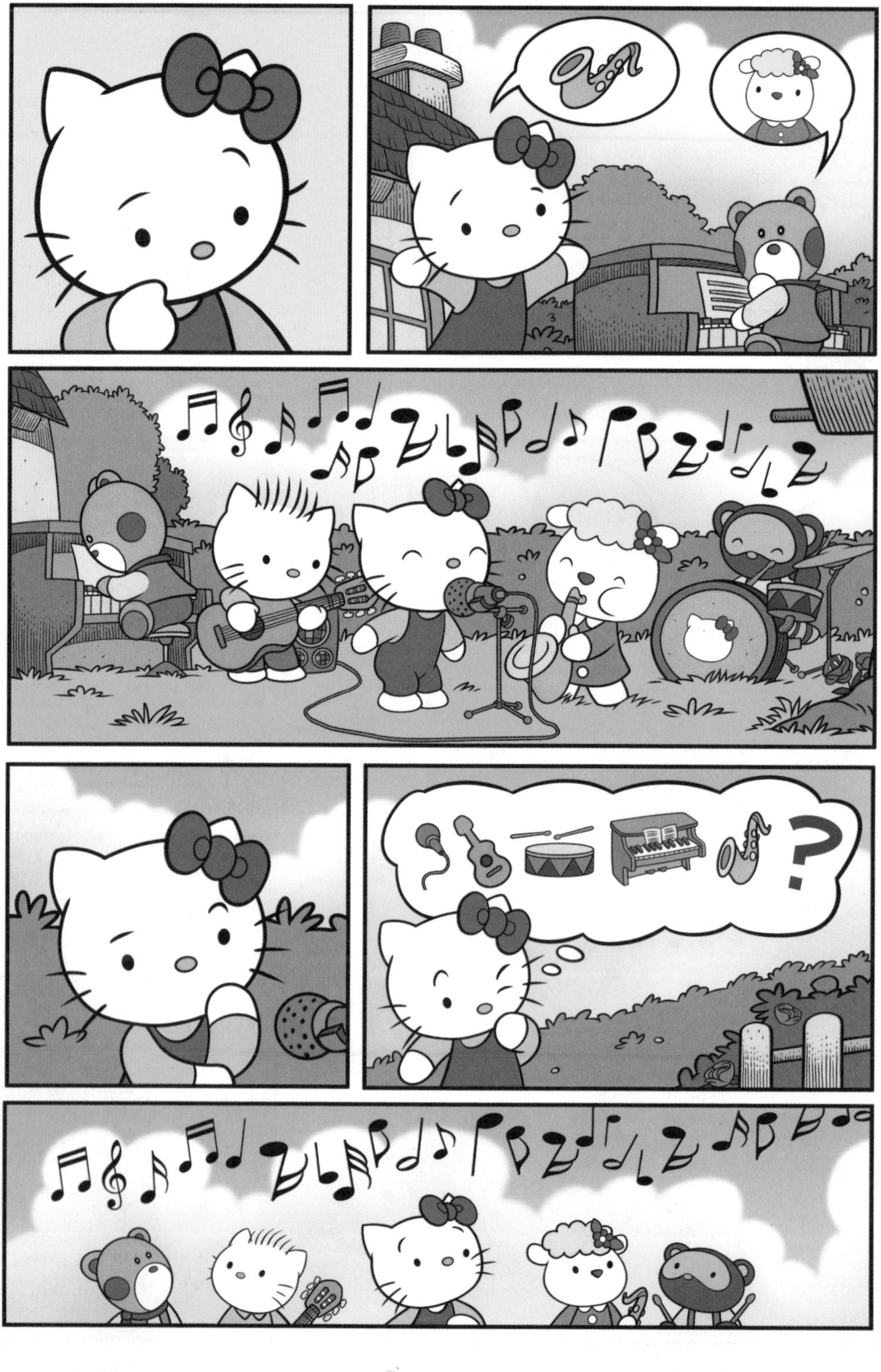

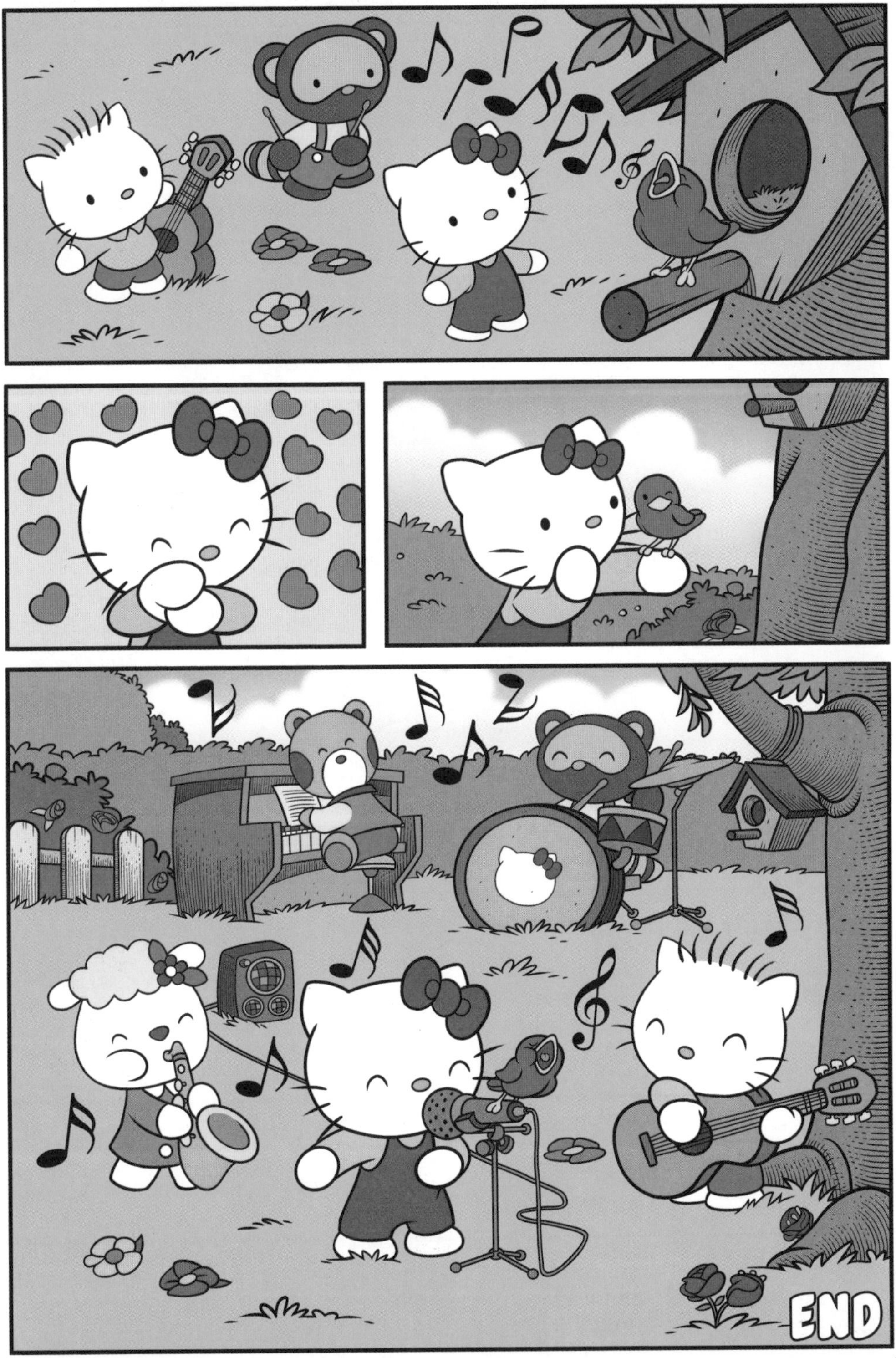
END

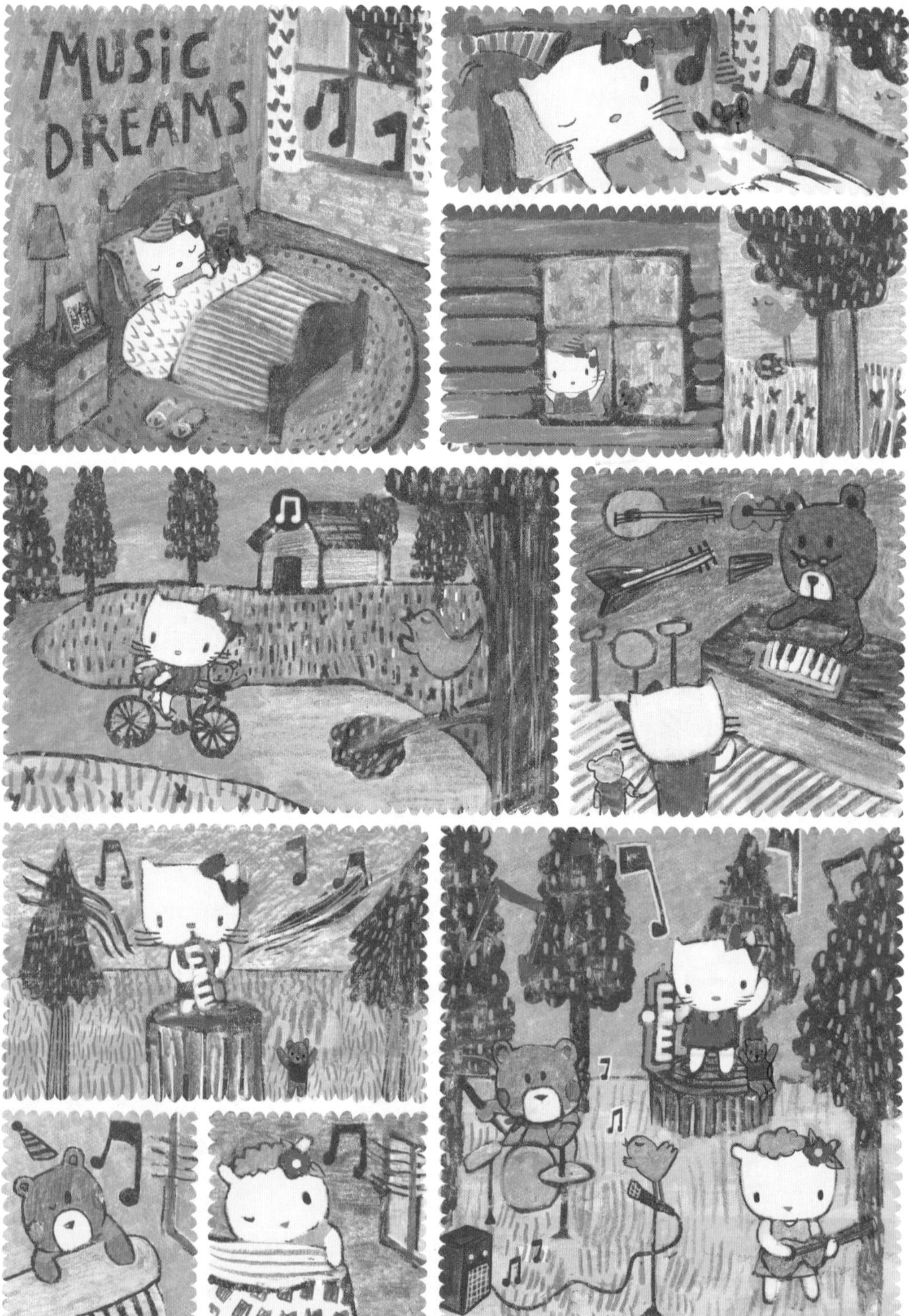
MUSIC DREAMS

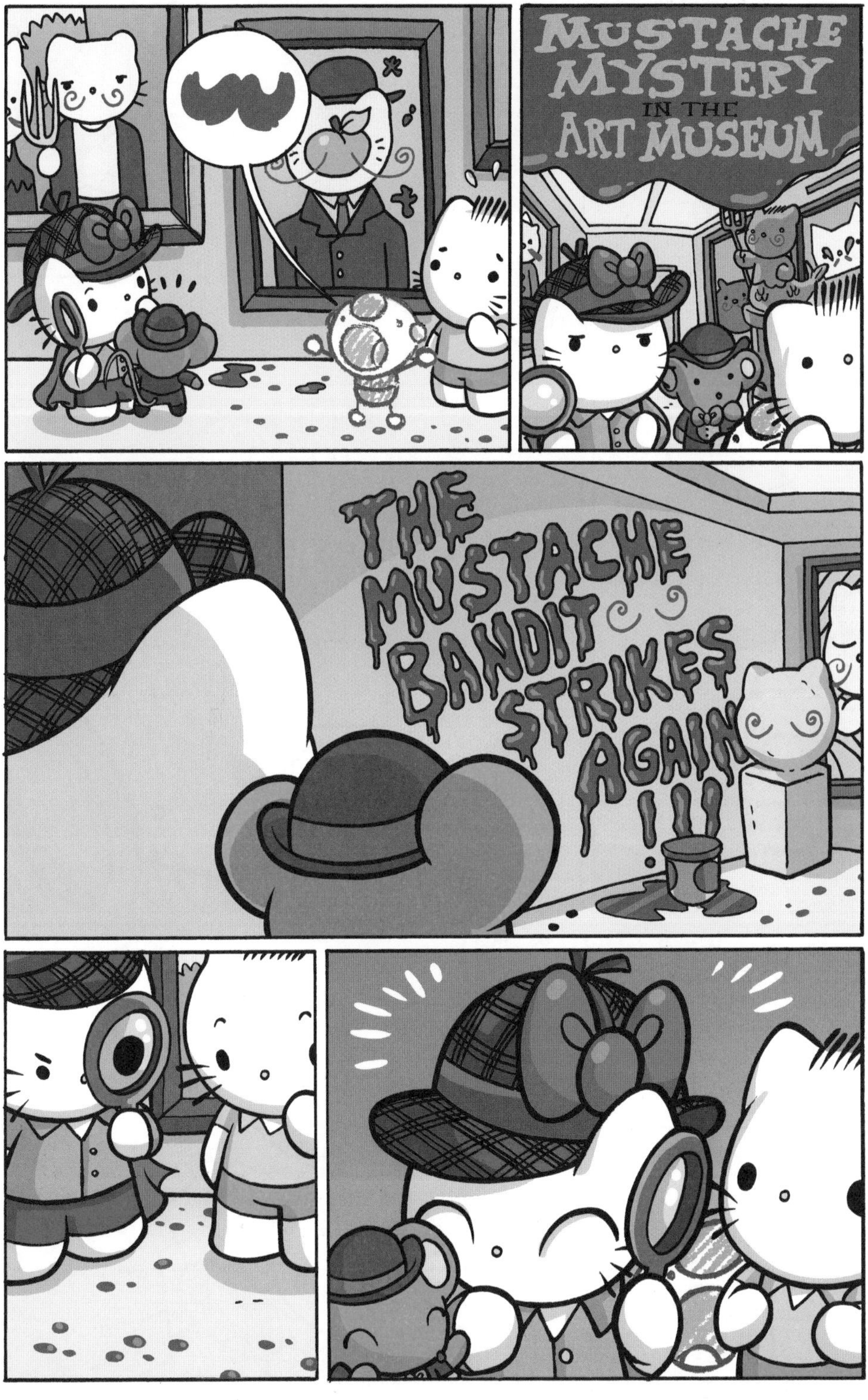
MUSTACHE MYSTERY IN THE ART MUSEUM
THE MUSTACHE BANDIT STRIKES AGAIN !!!

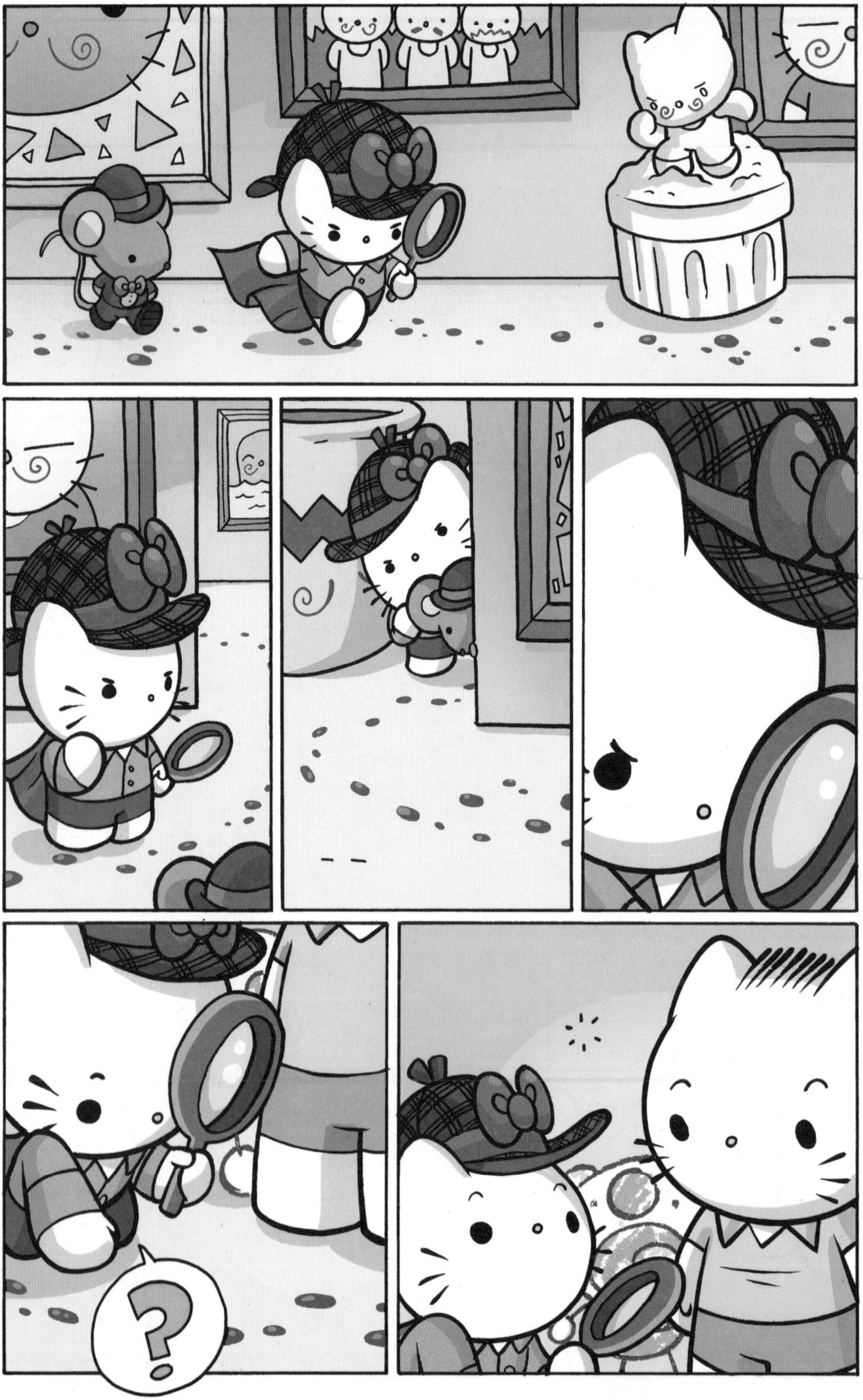
?

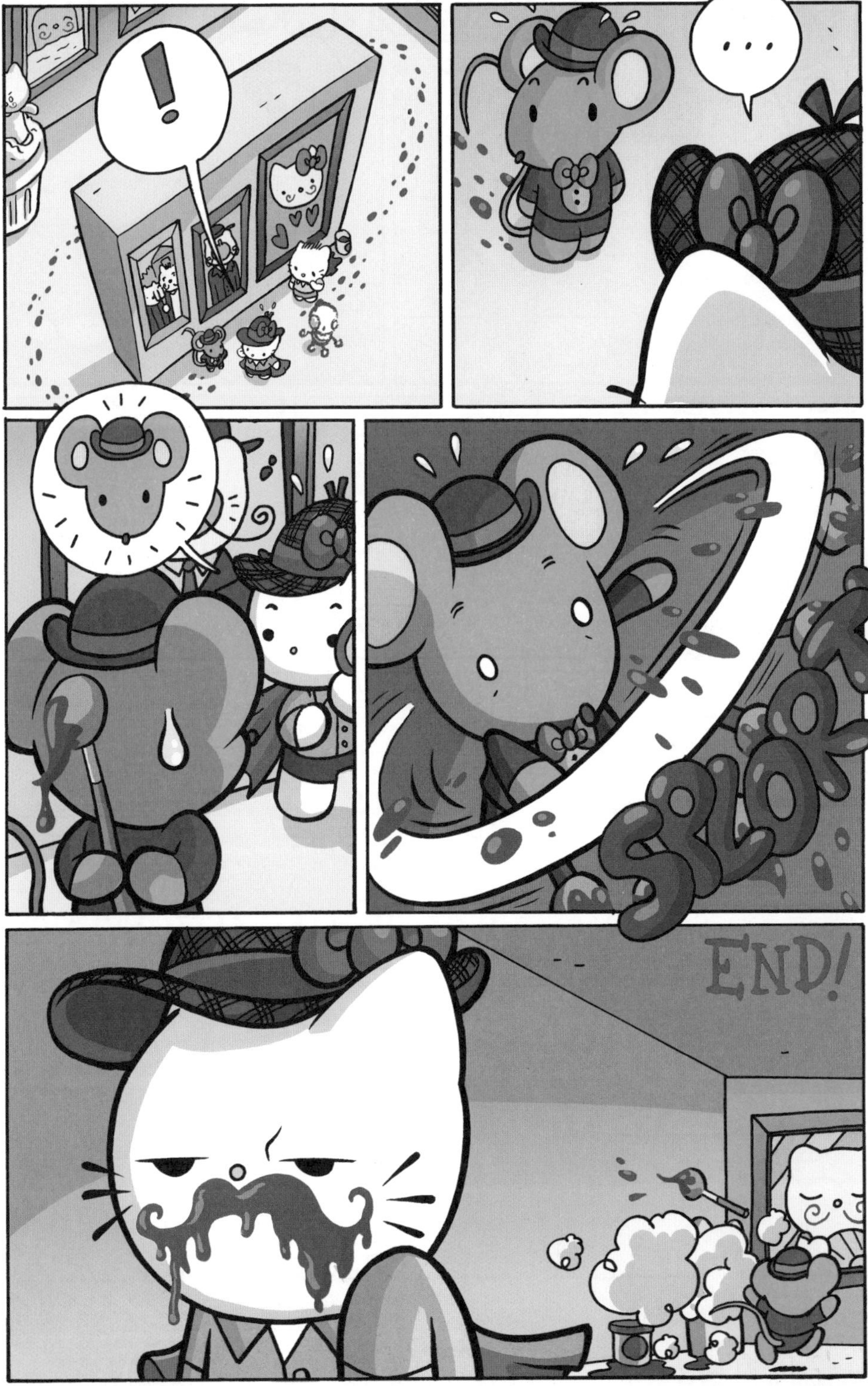
!
...
SPLORT
END!

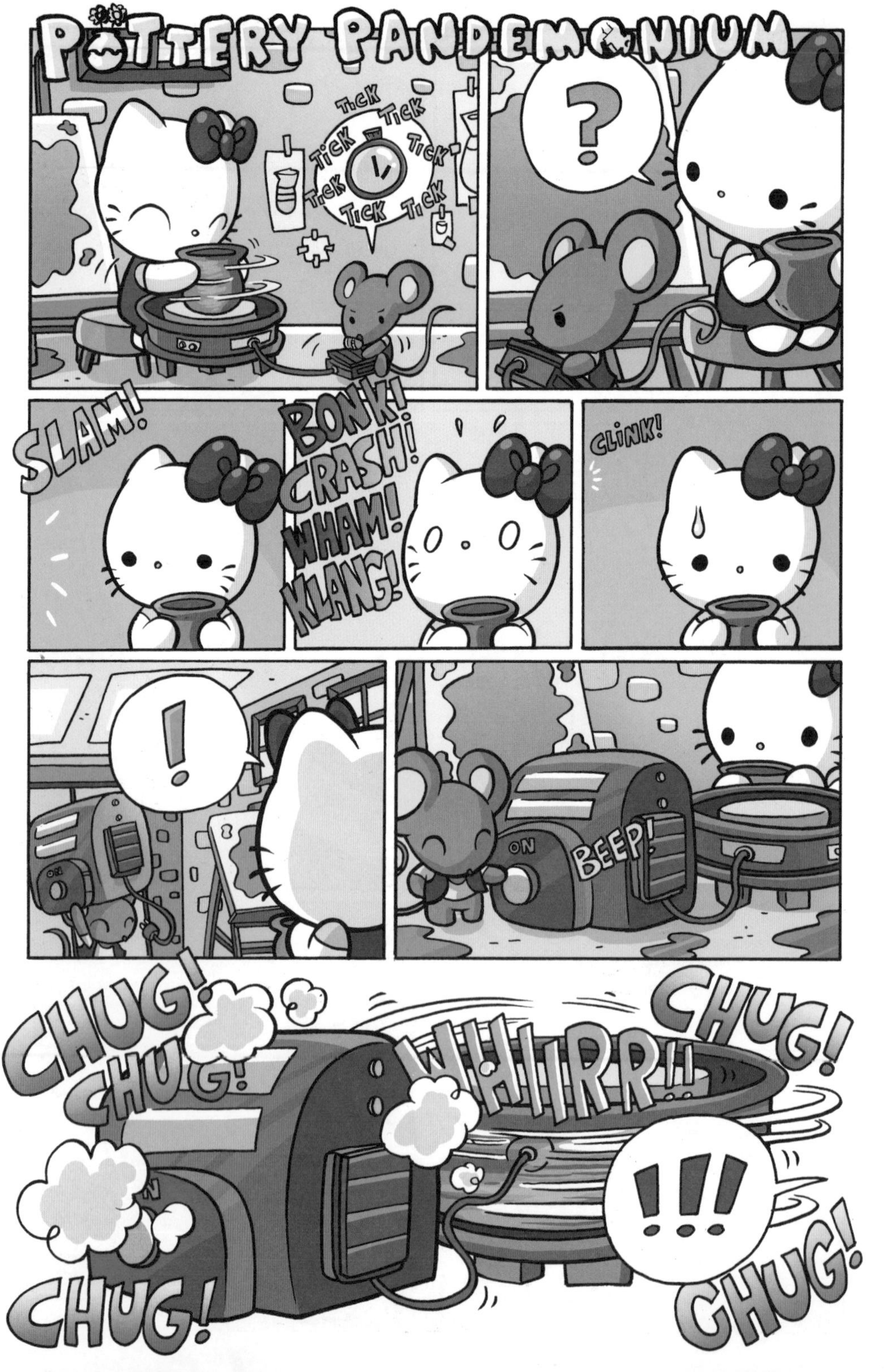
POTTERY PANDEMONIUM
TICK TICK TICK TICK TICK TICK TICK TICK
?
SLAM!
BONK! CRASH! WHAM! KLANG!
CLINK!
!
ON
BEEP!
CHUG! CHUG!
WHIIRR!!
CHUG!
CHUG!
!!!
CHUG!

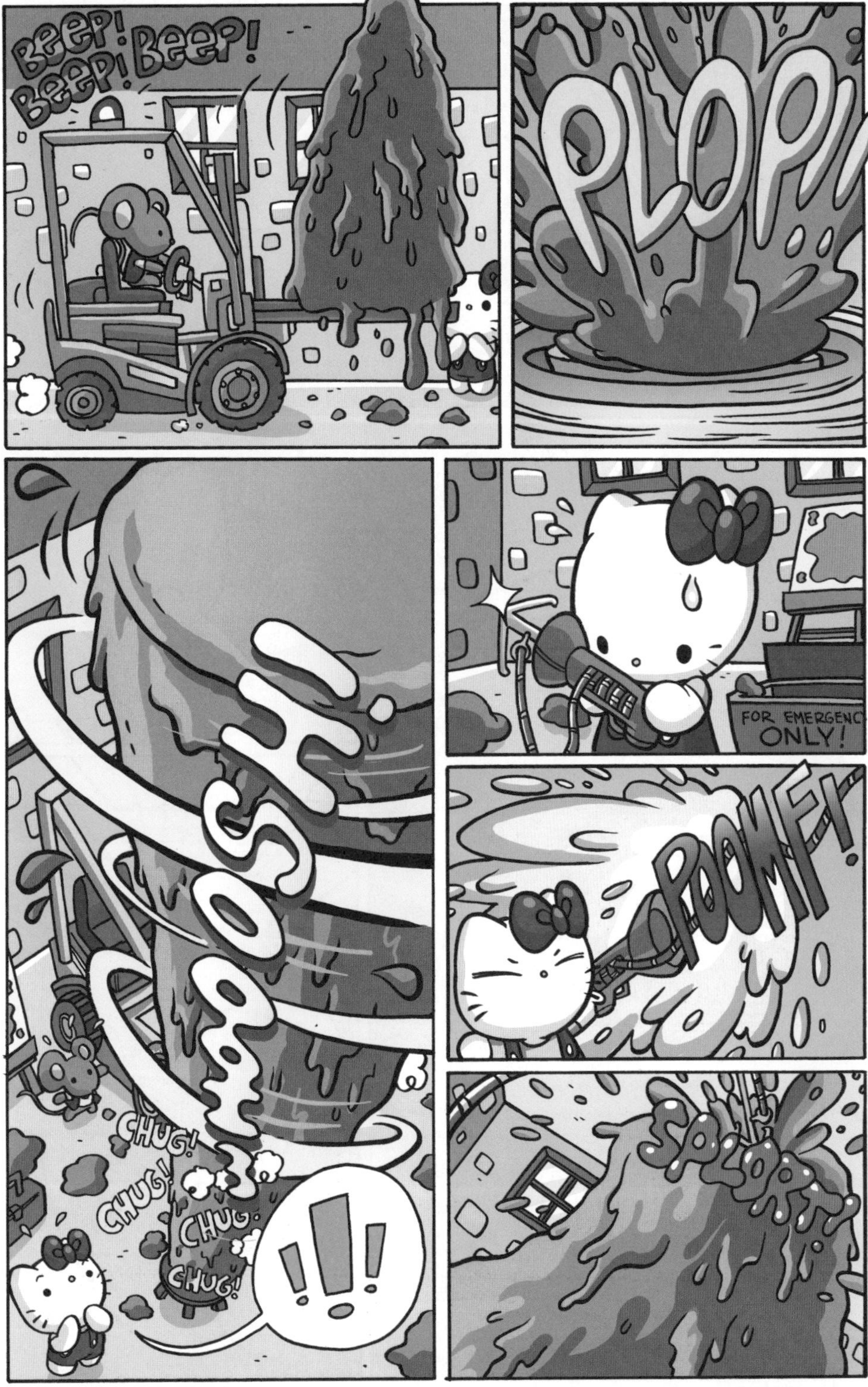
BEEP! BEEP! BEEP!
PLOP!!
WHOOSH!
CHUG! CHUG! CHUG! CHUG!
!!!
FOR EMERGENCY ONLY!
POOMF!
SPLORT!

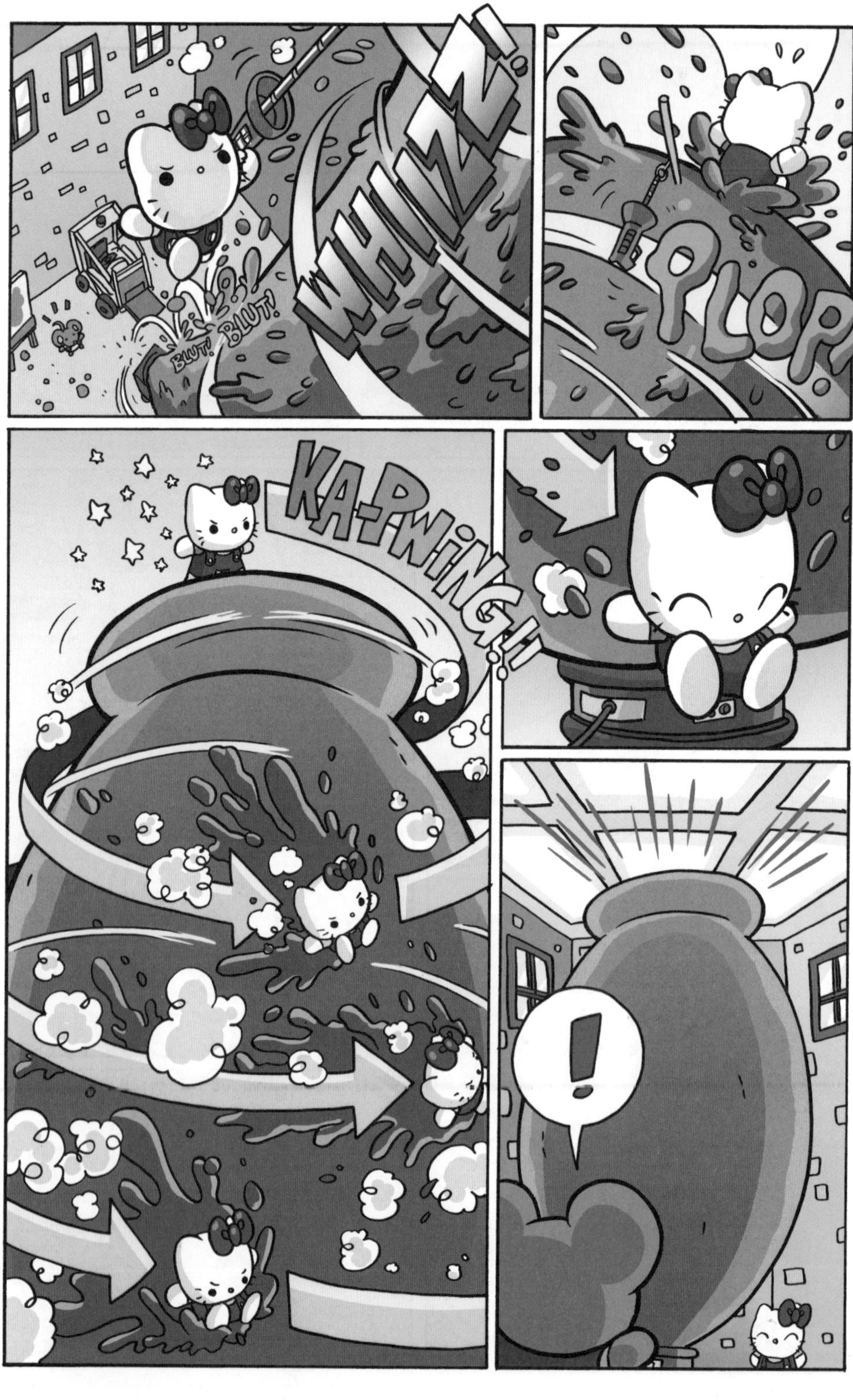
BLUT! BLUT!
WHIIZ!
PLOP!
KA-PWING!!
!

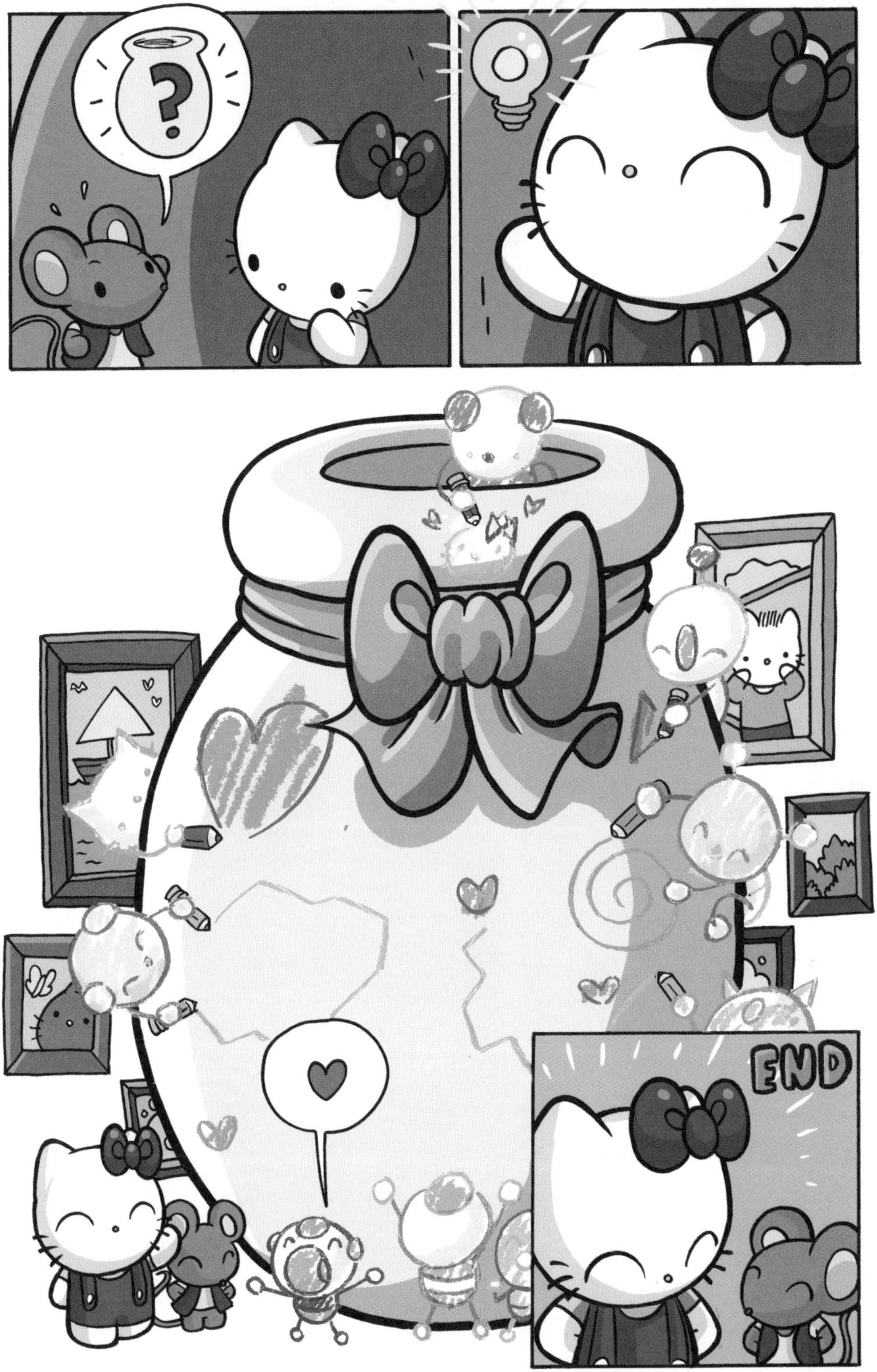
?
END

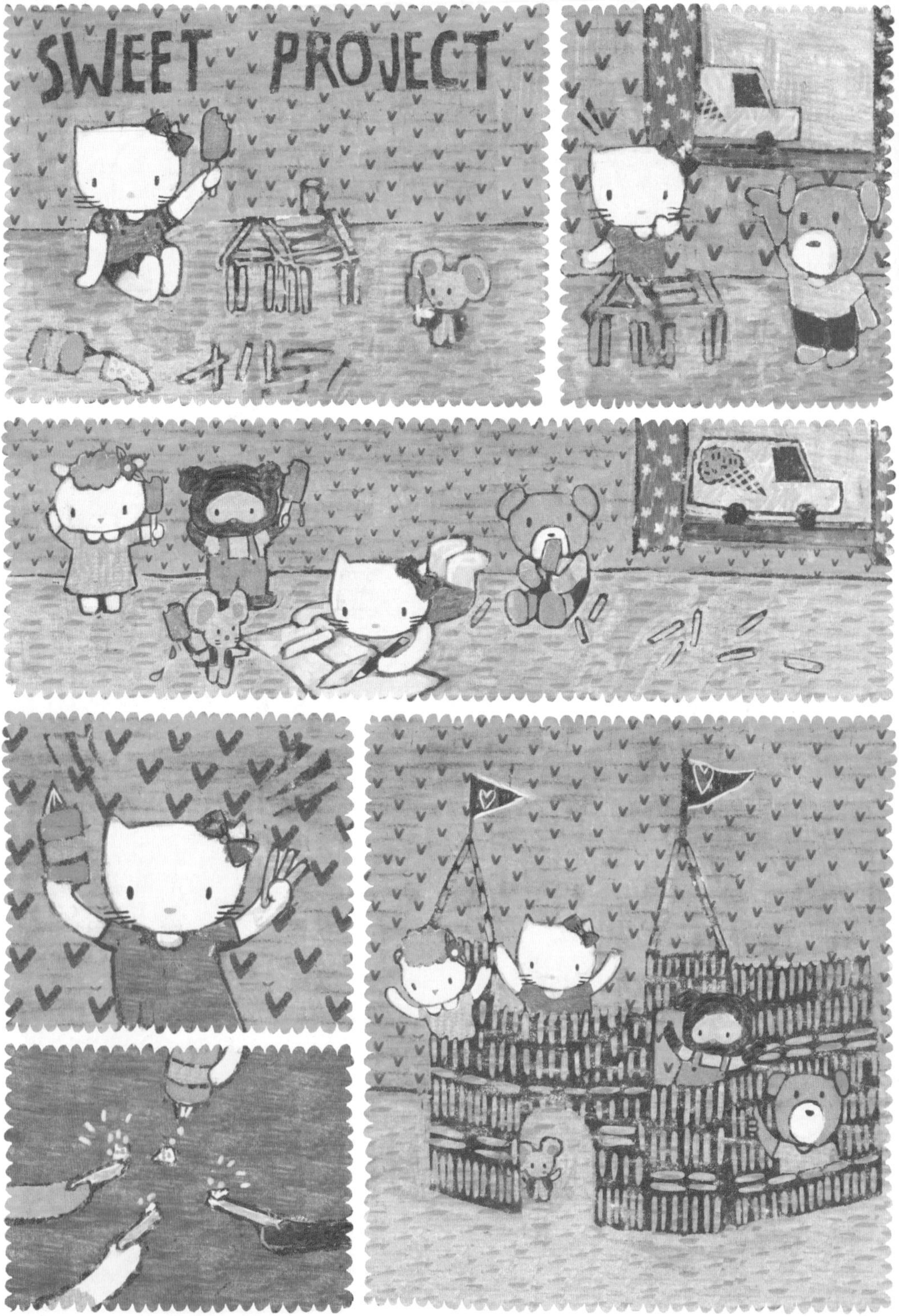
SWEET PROJECT

PAINTINGS

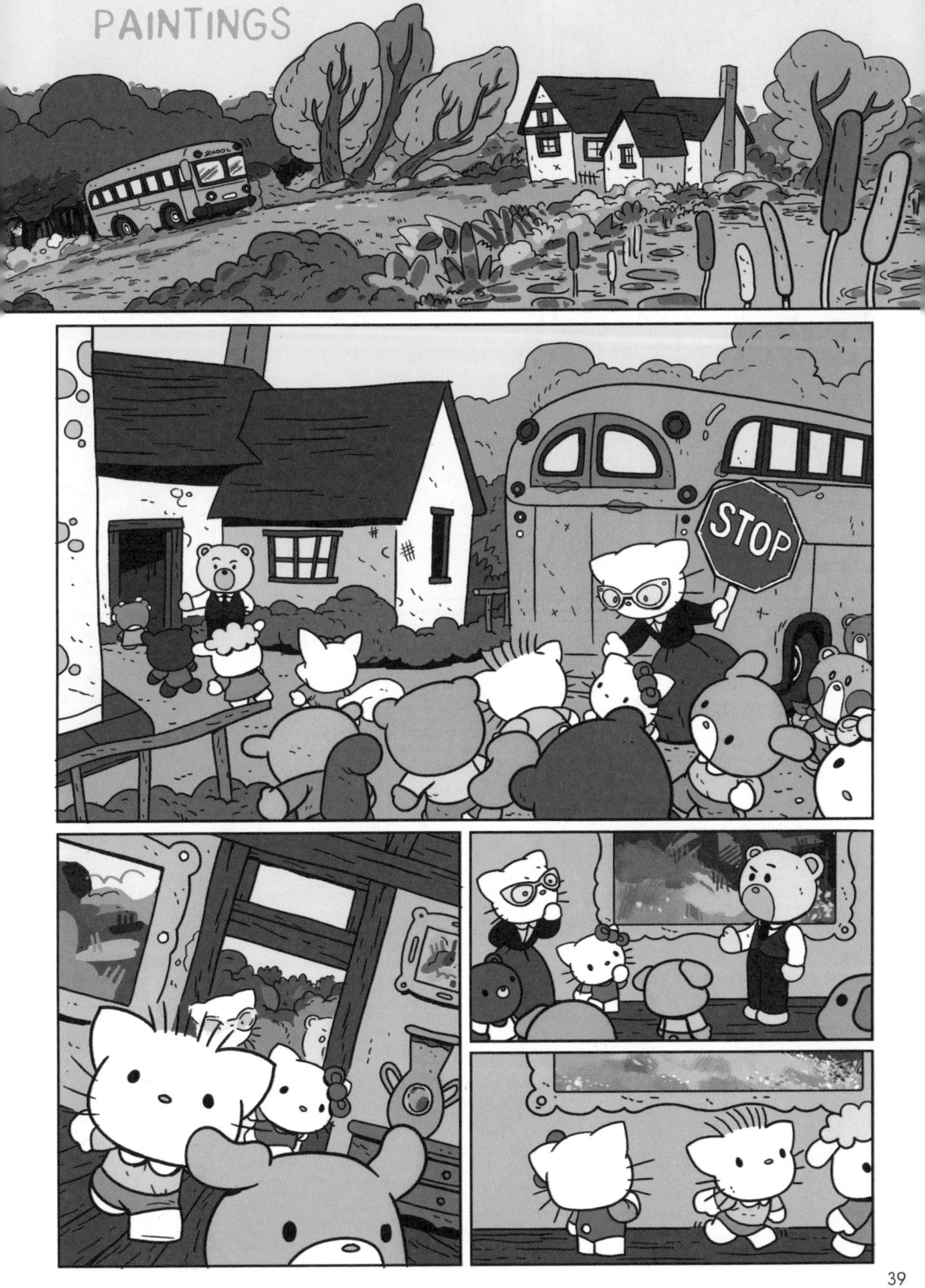
SCHOOL
STOP

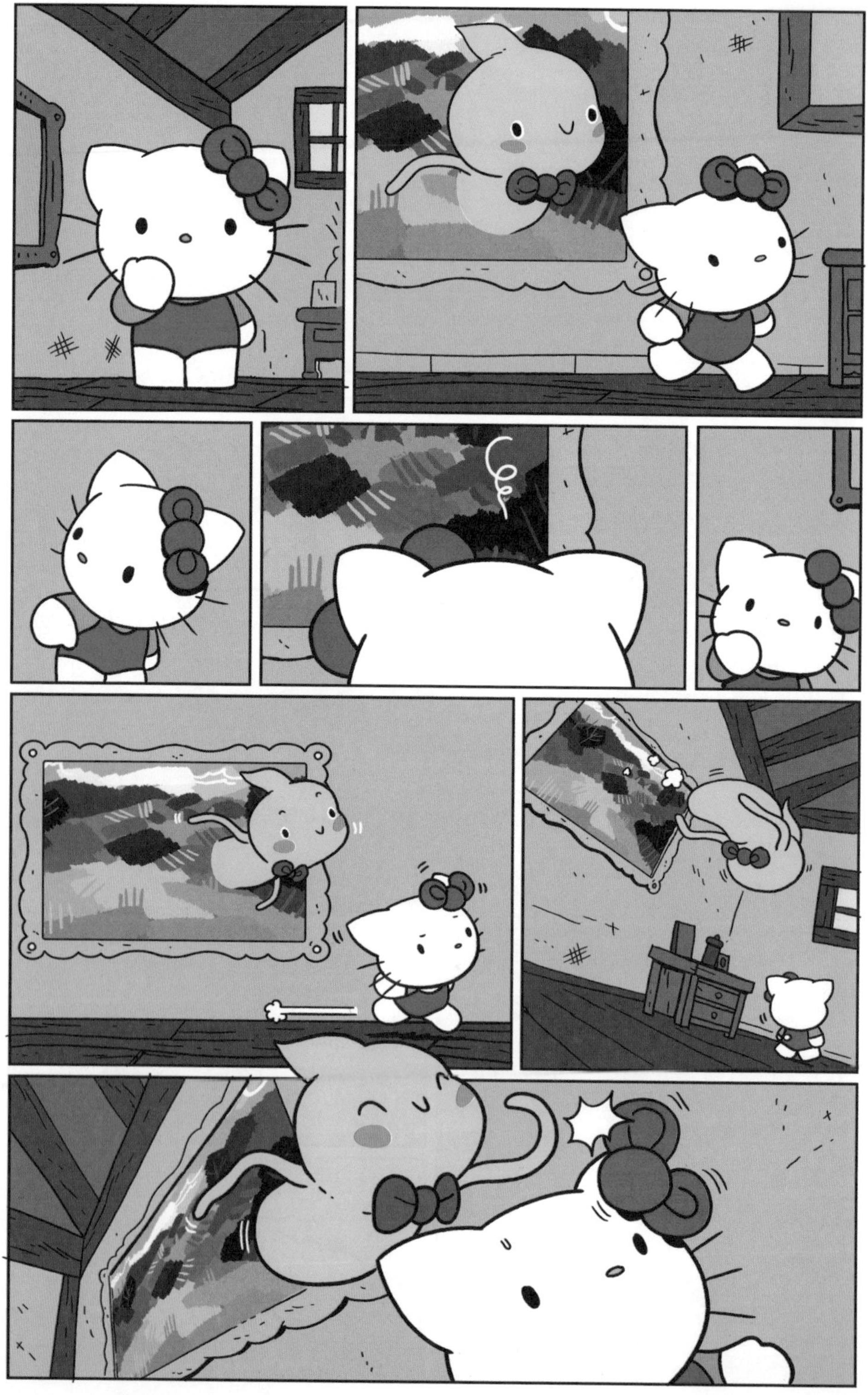

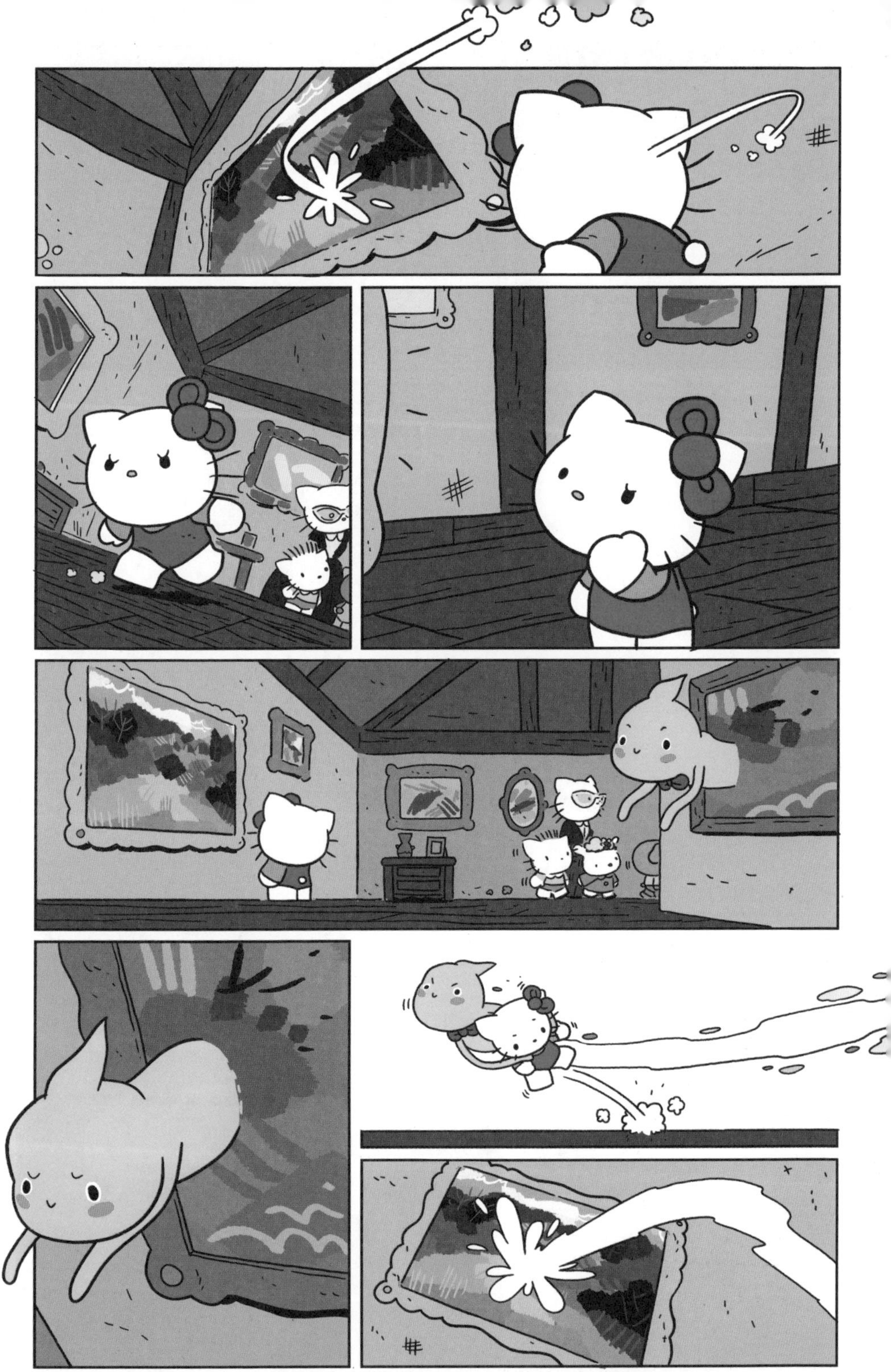

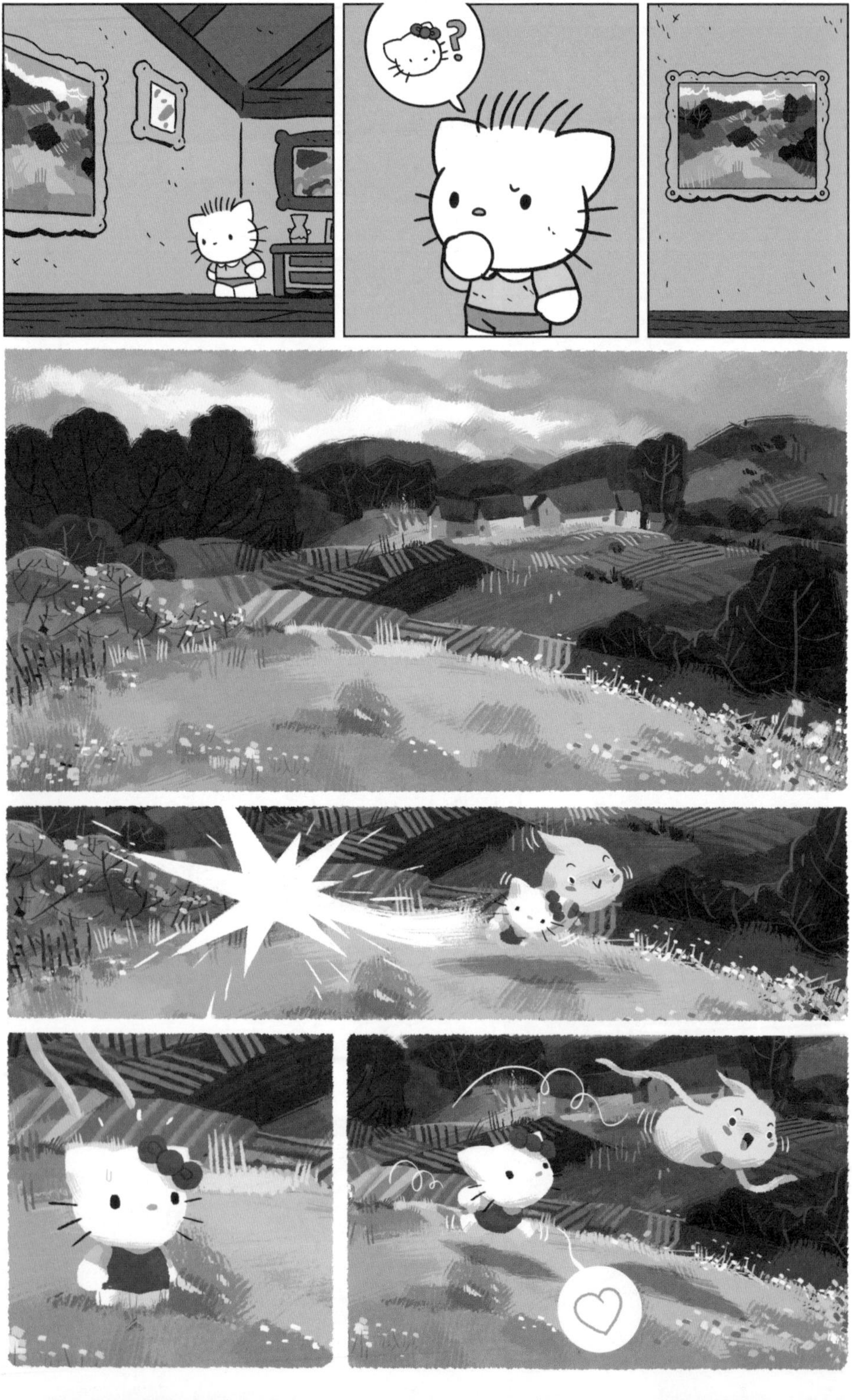

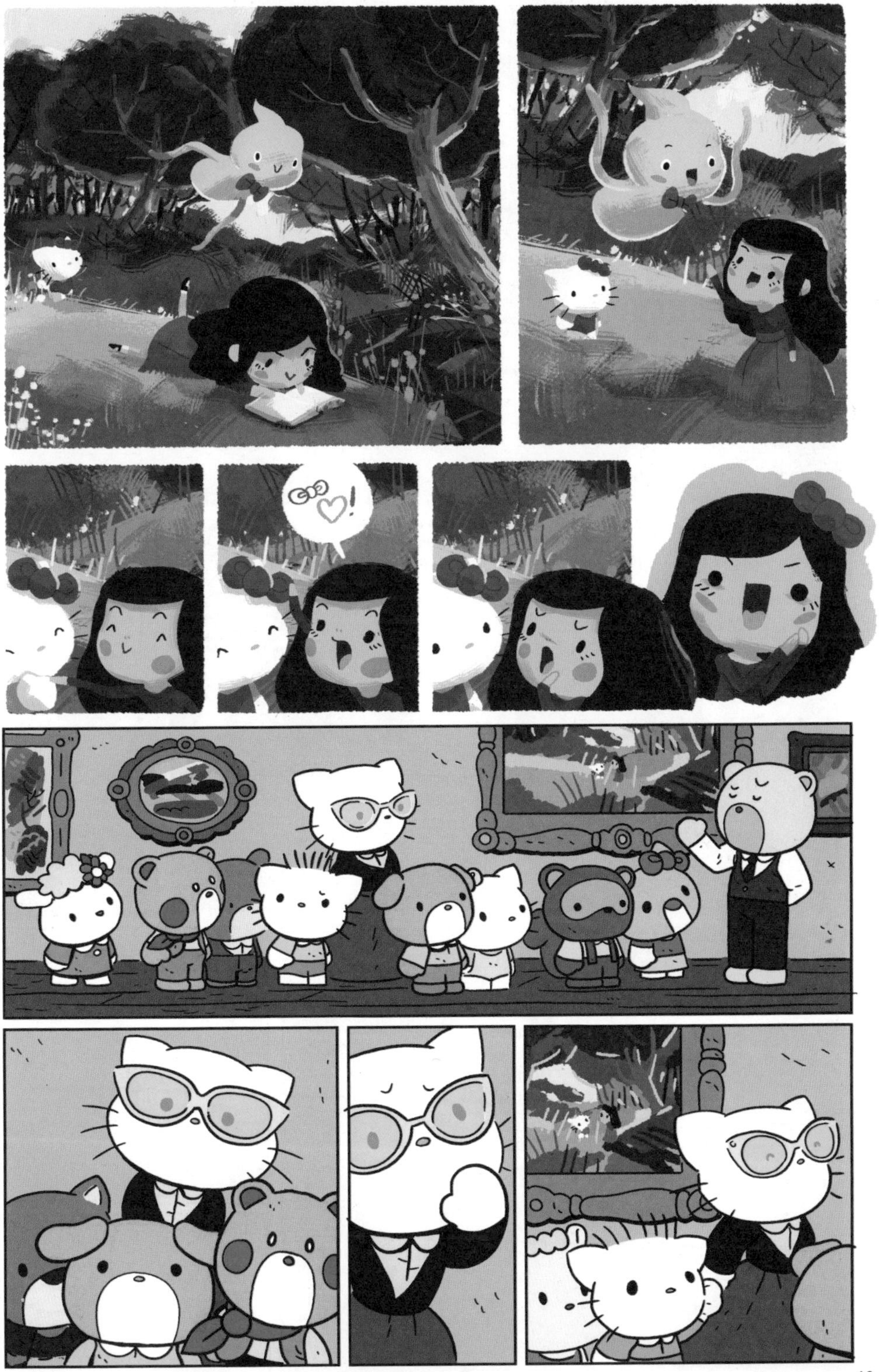

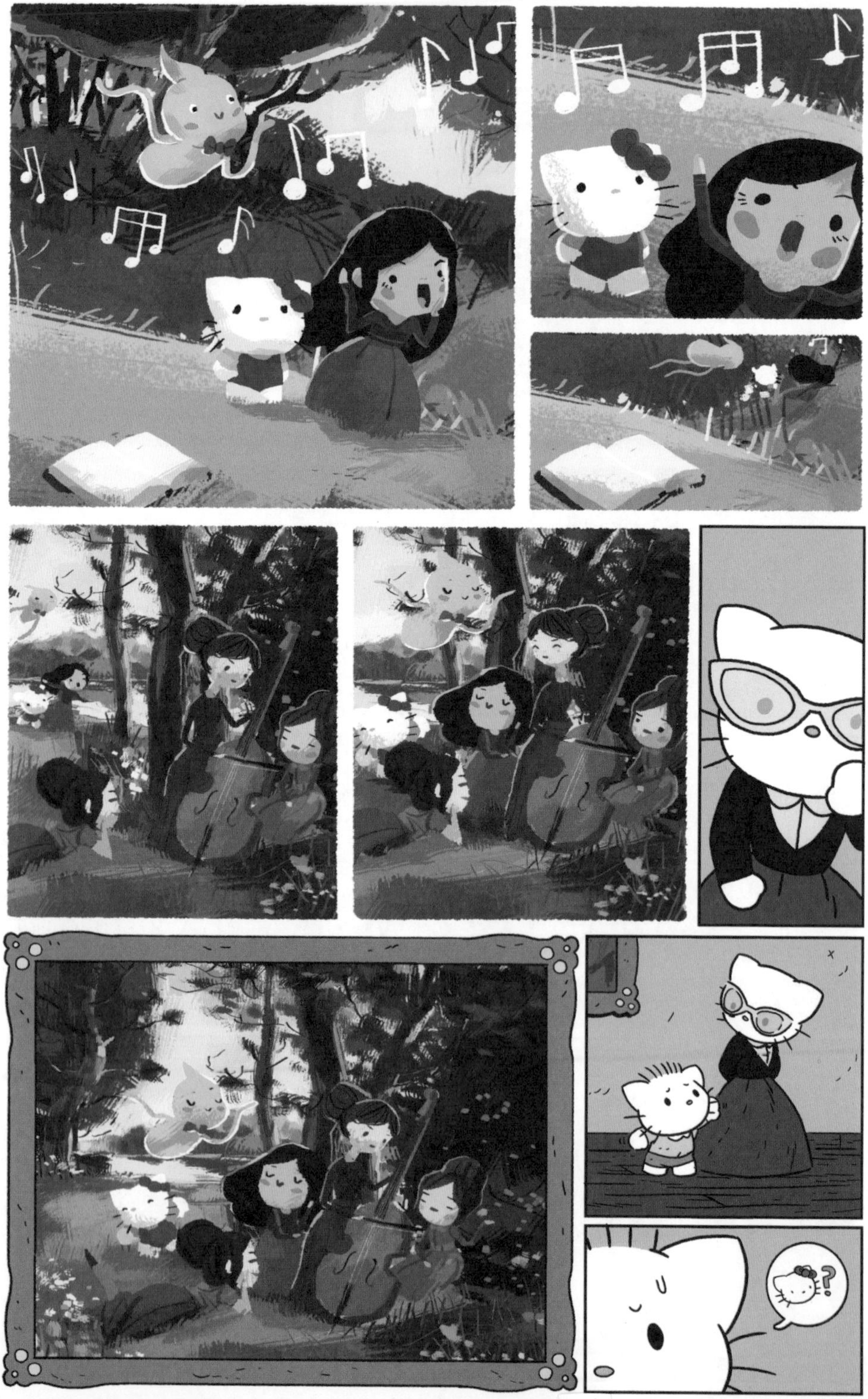
?

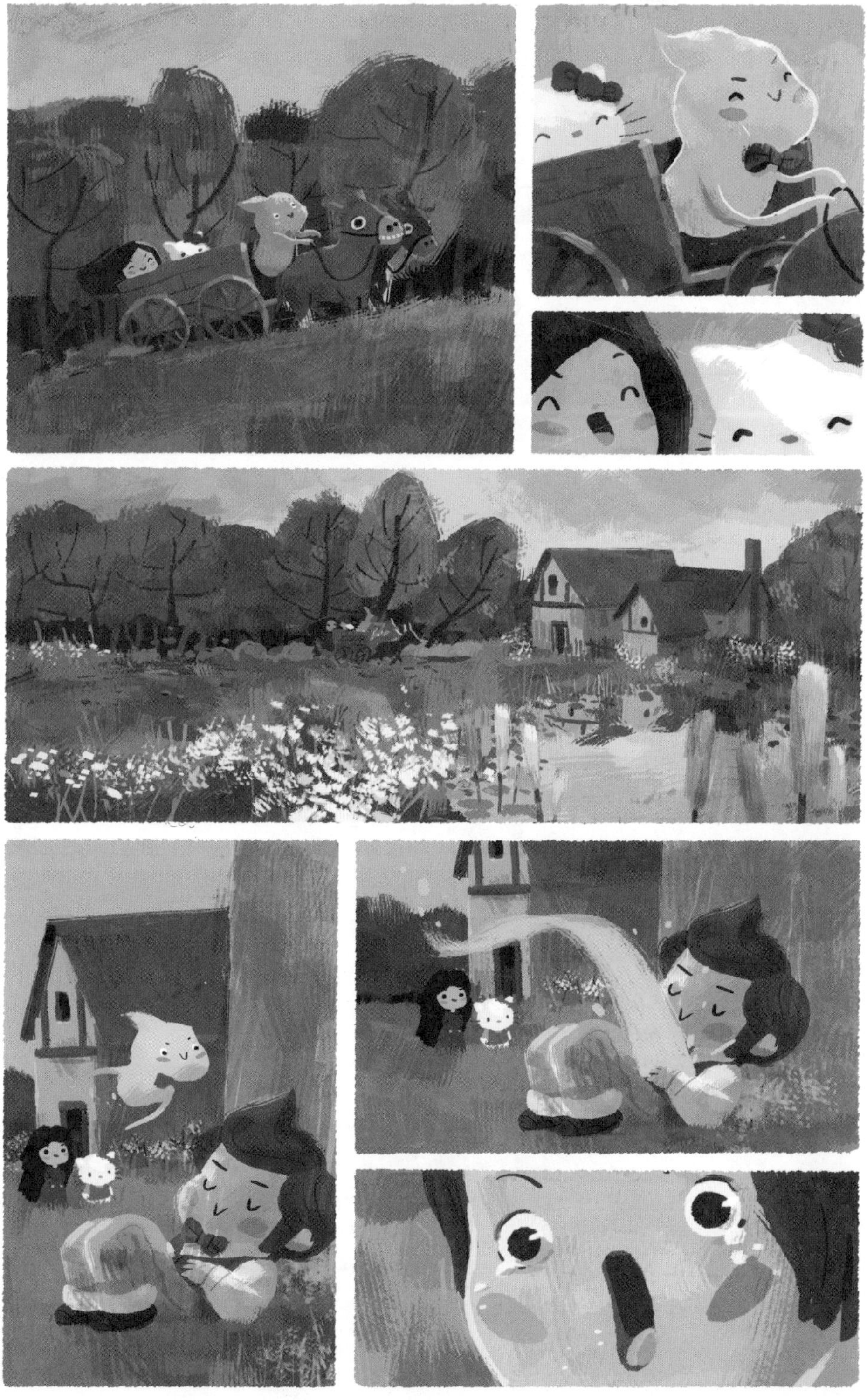

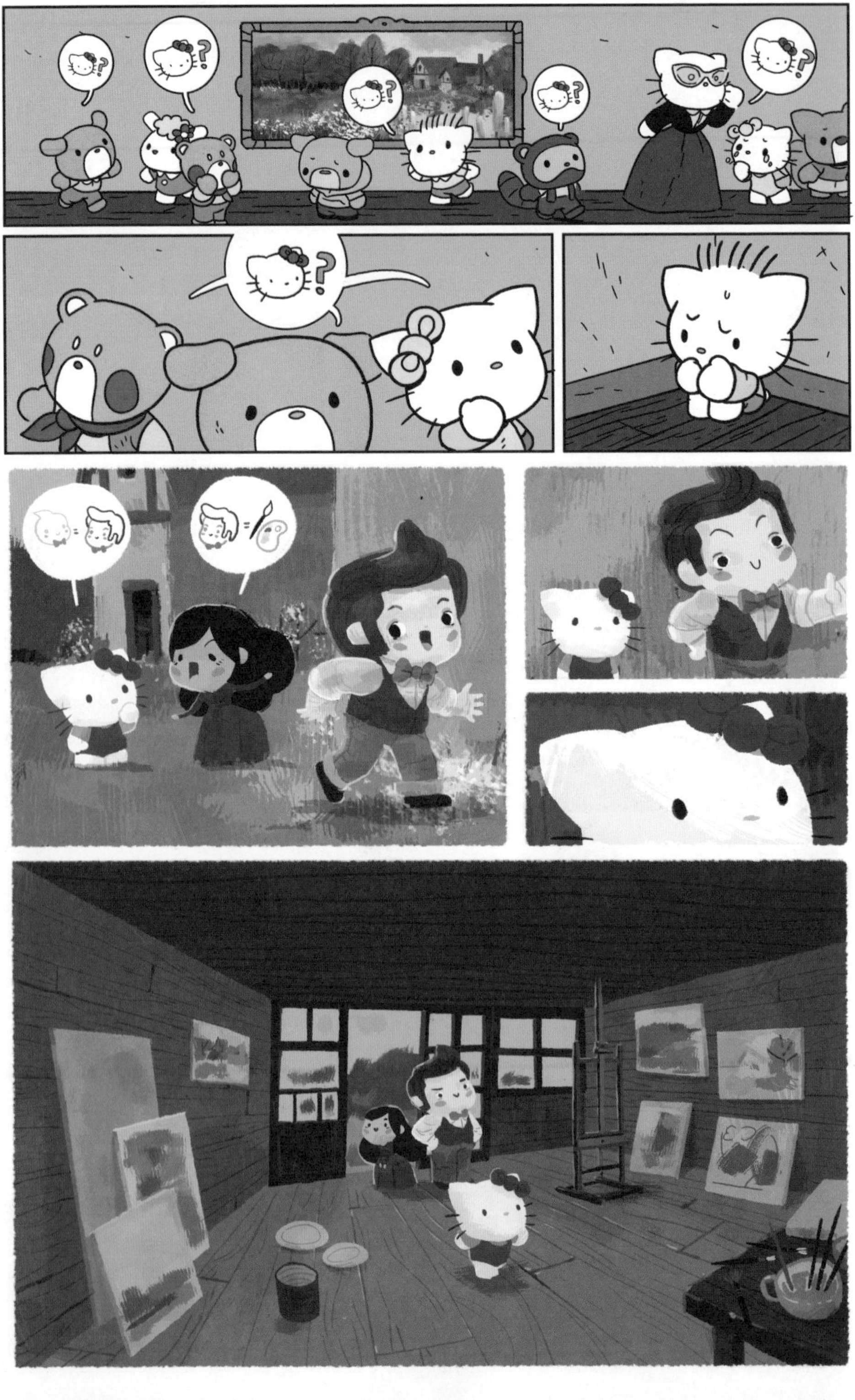

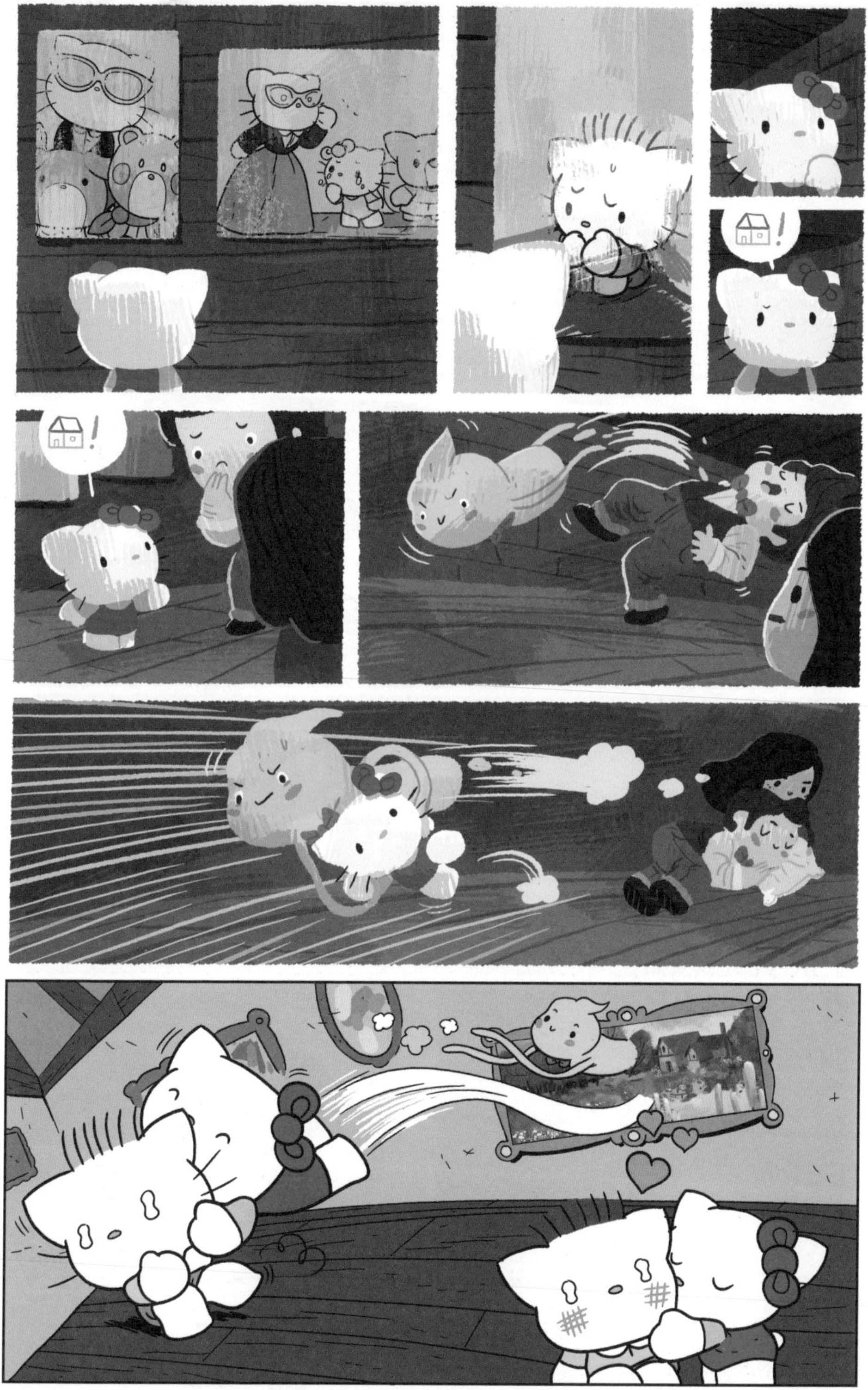

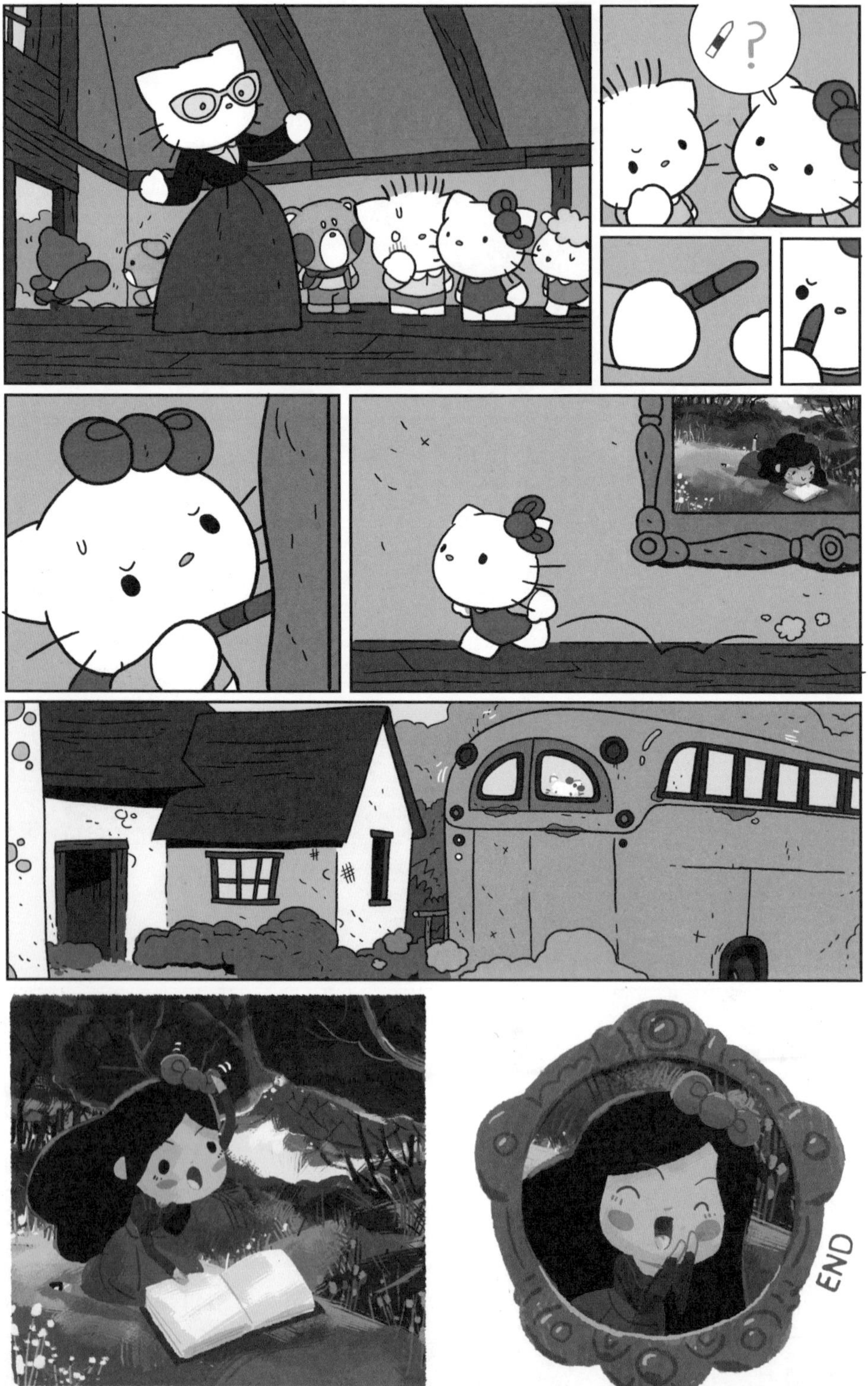

?
END

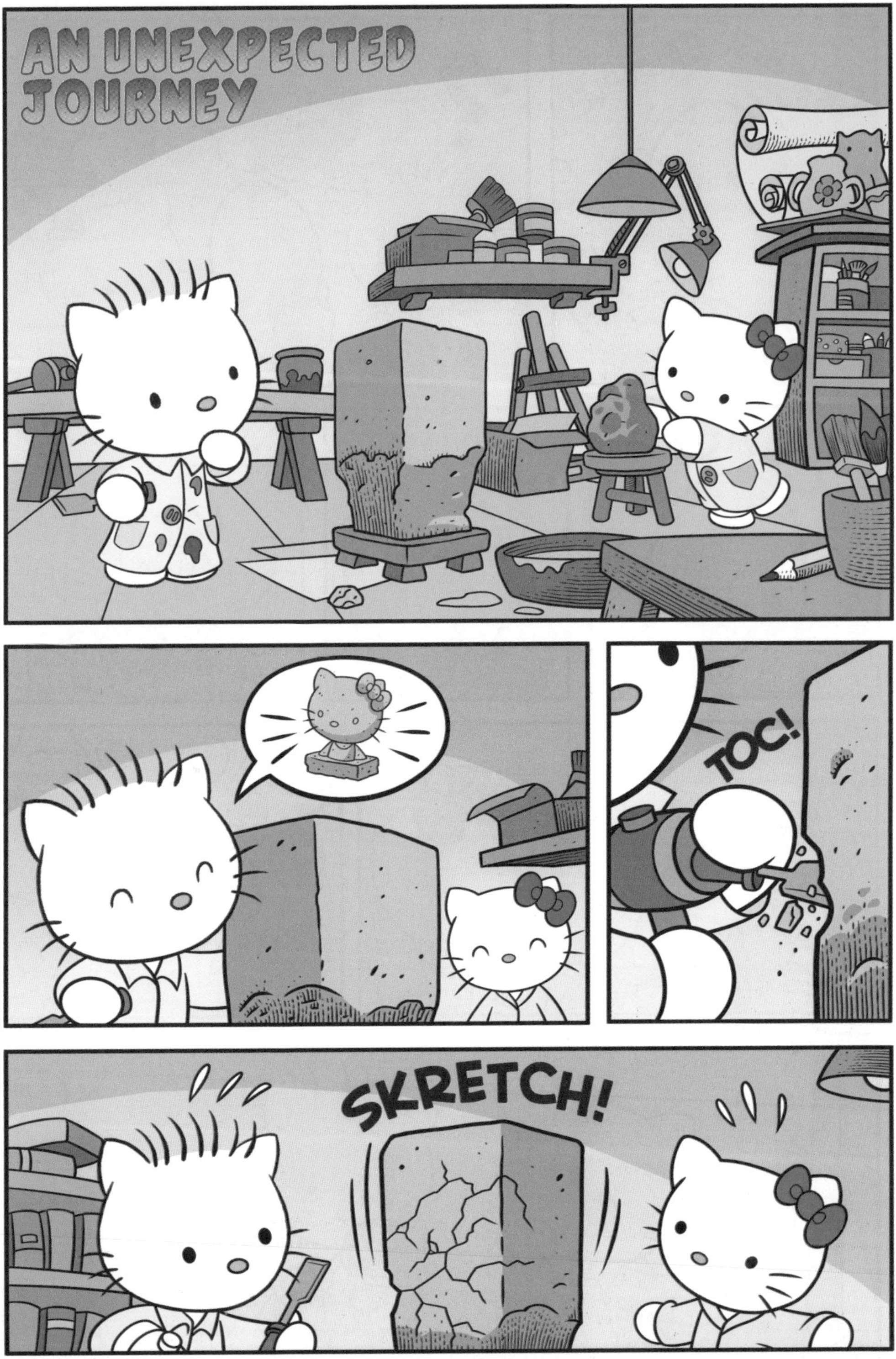
AN UNEXPECTED JOURNEY
TOC!
SKRETCH!

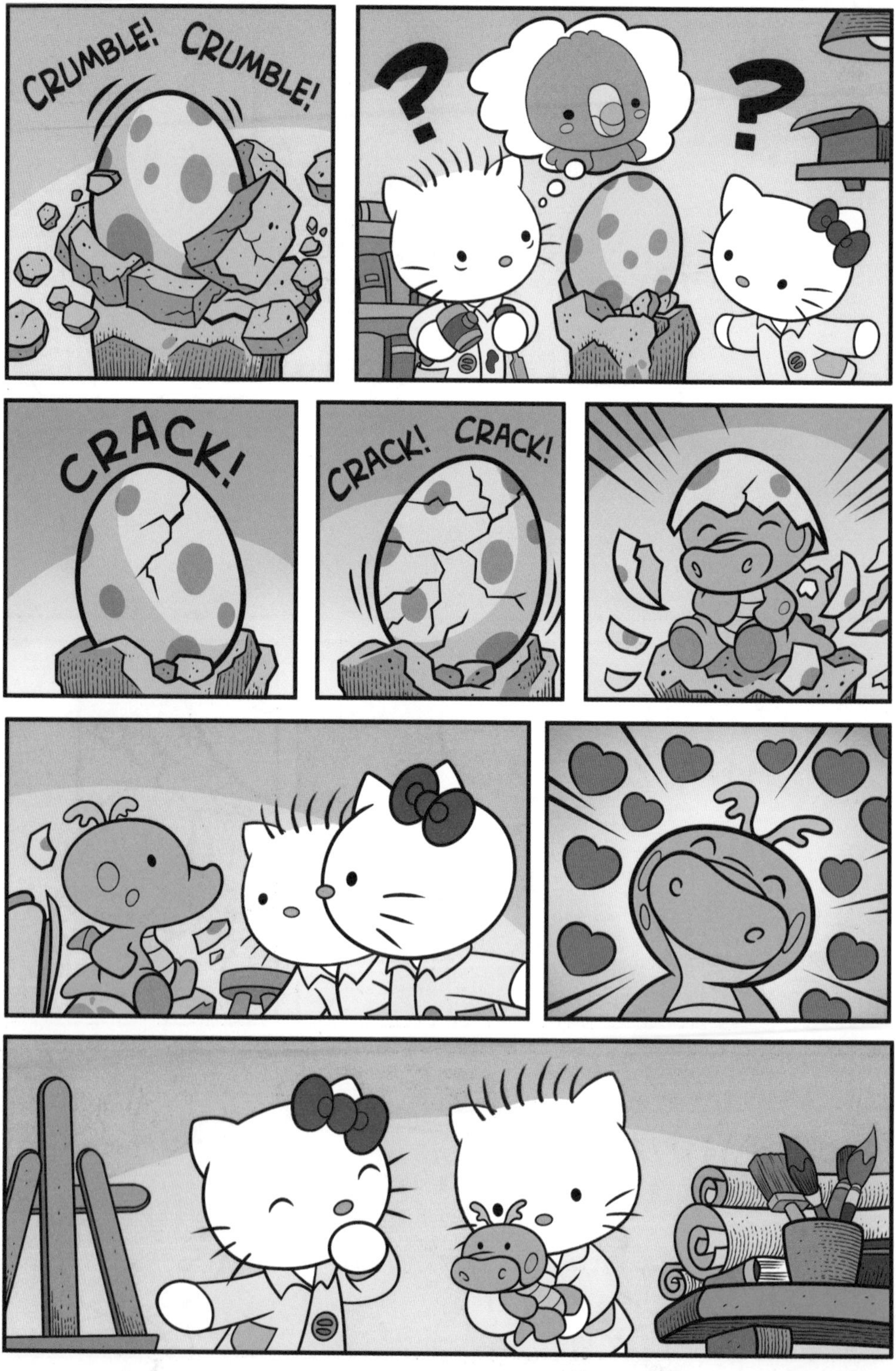
CRUMBLE! CRUMBLE!
CRACK!
CRACK! CRACK!

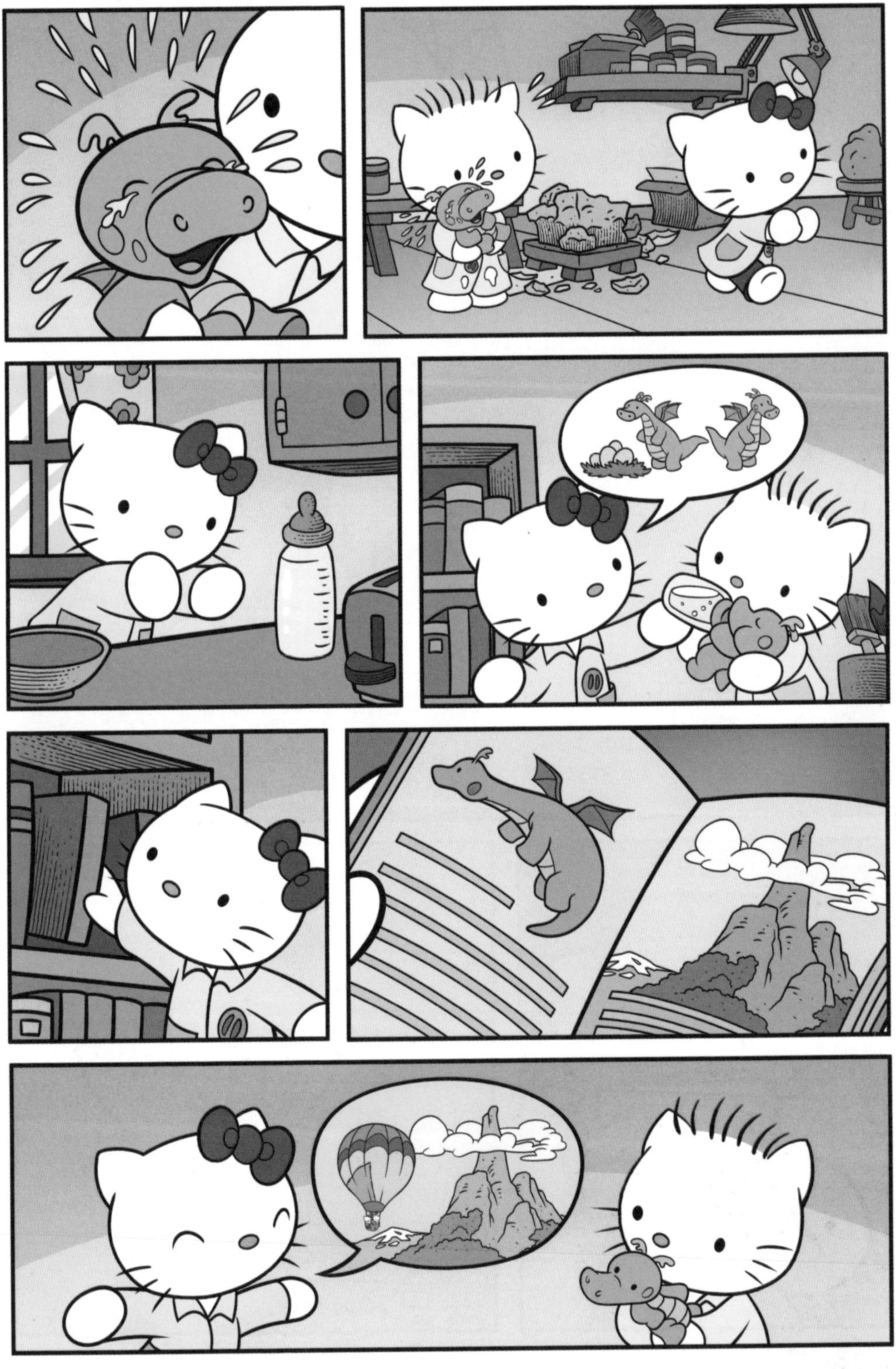

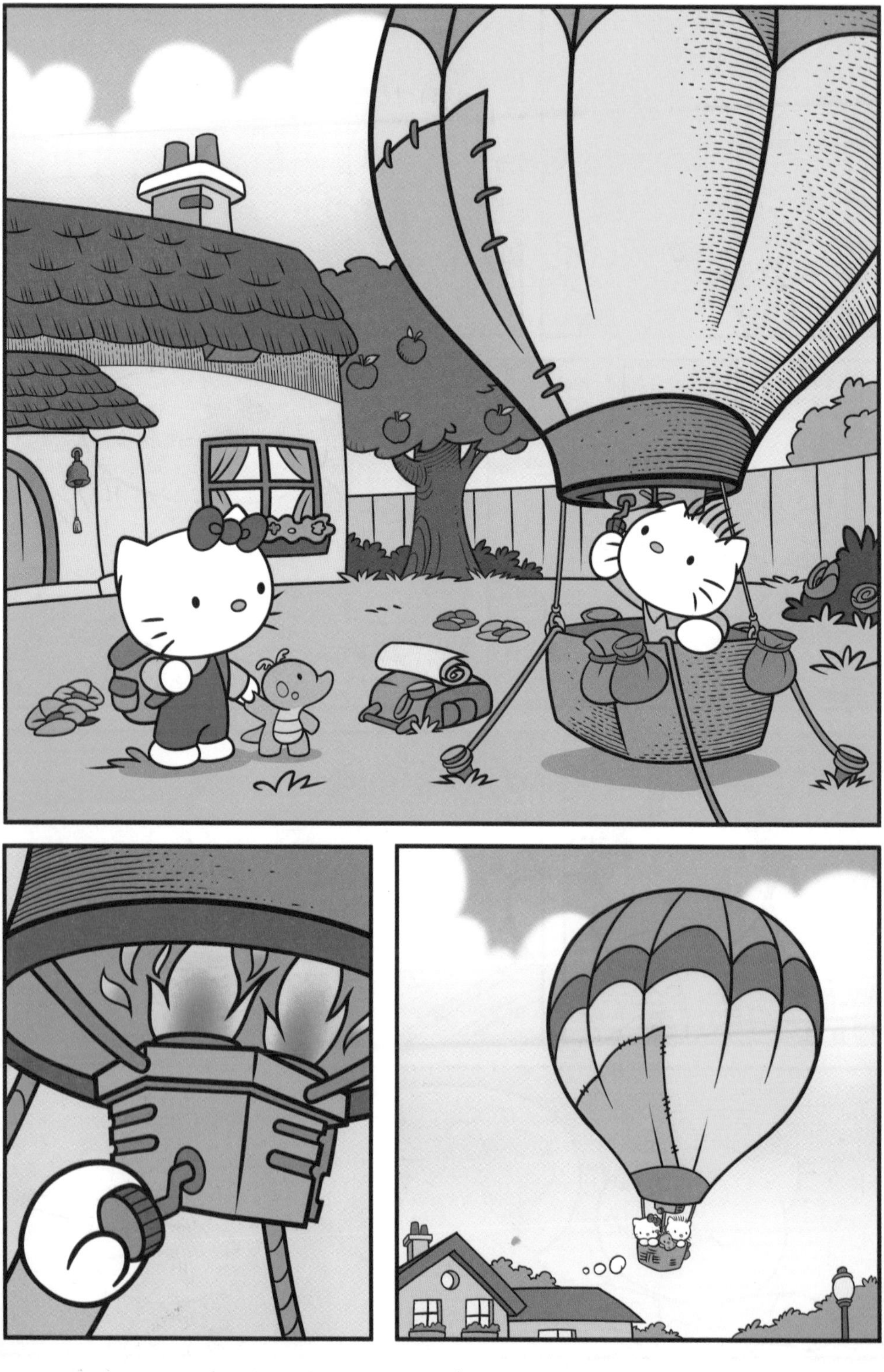

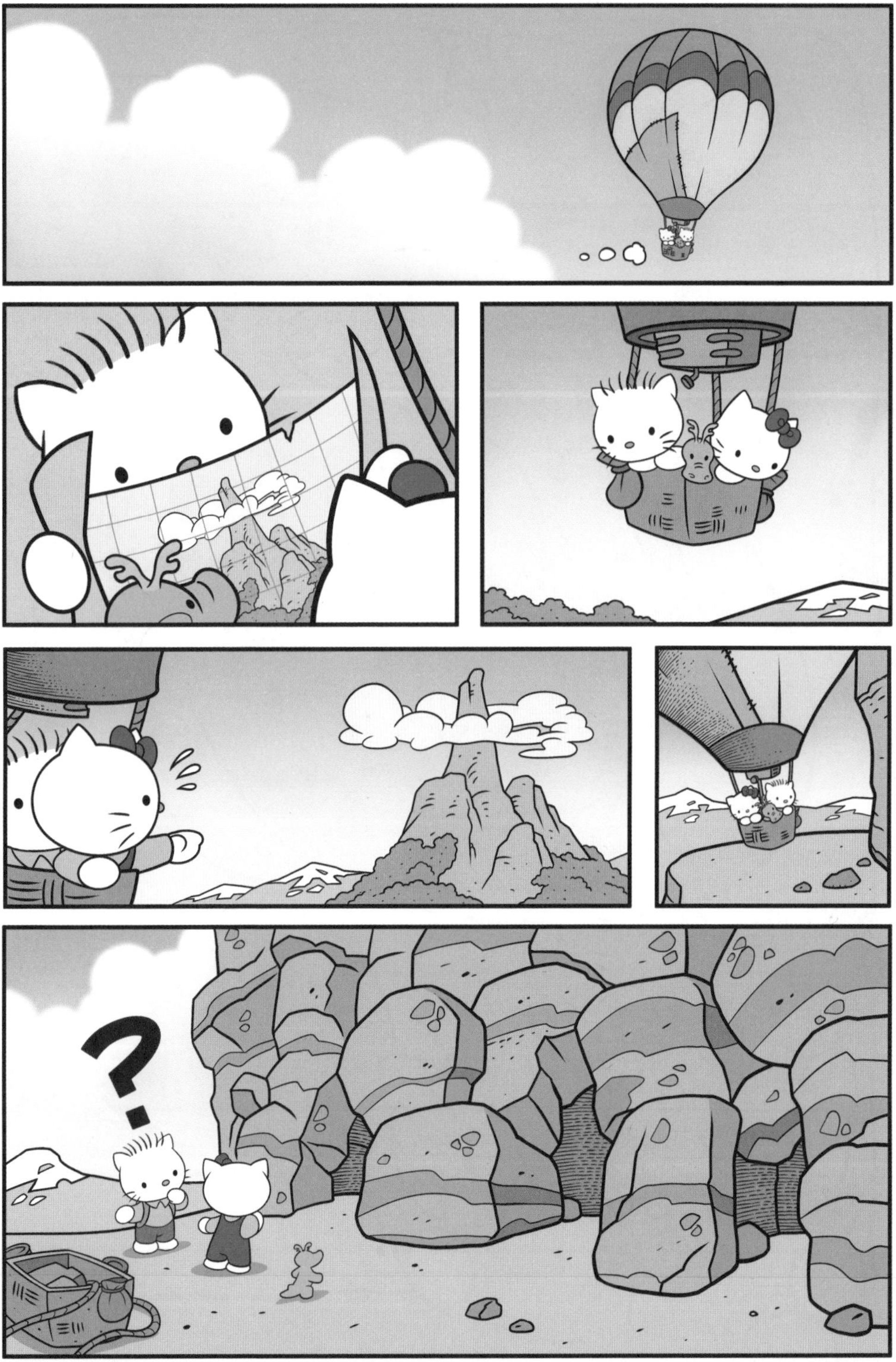
?

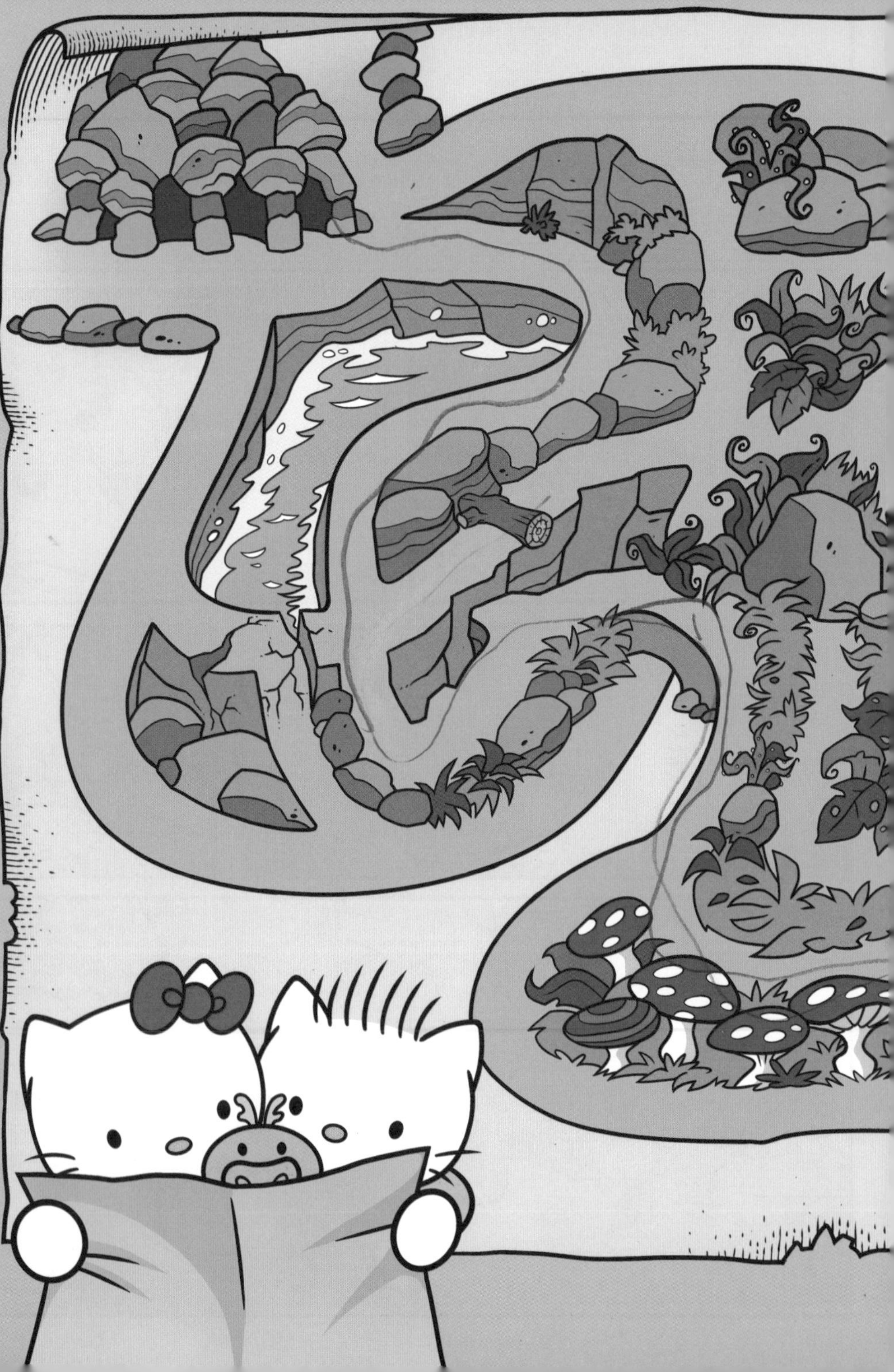

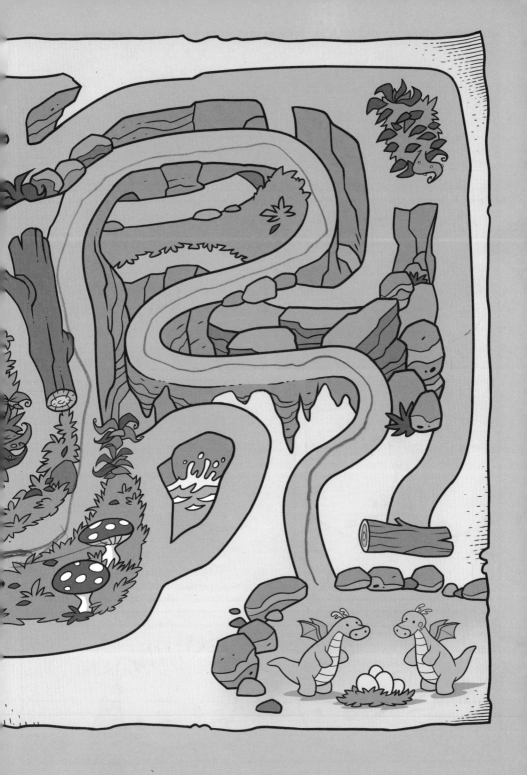

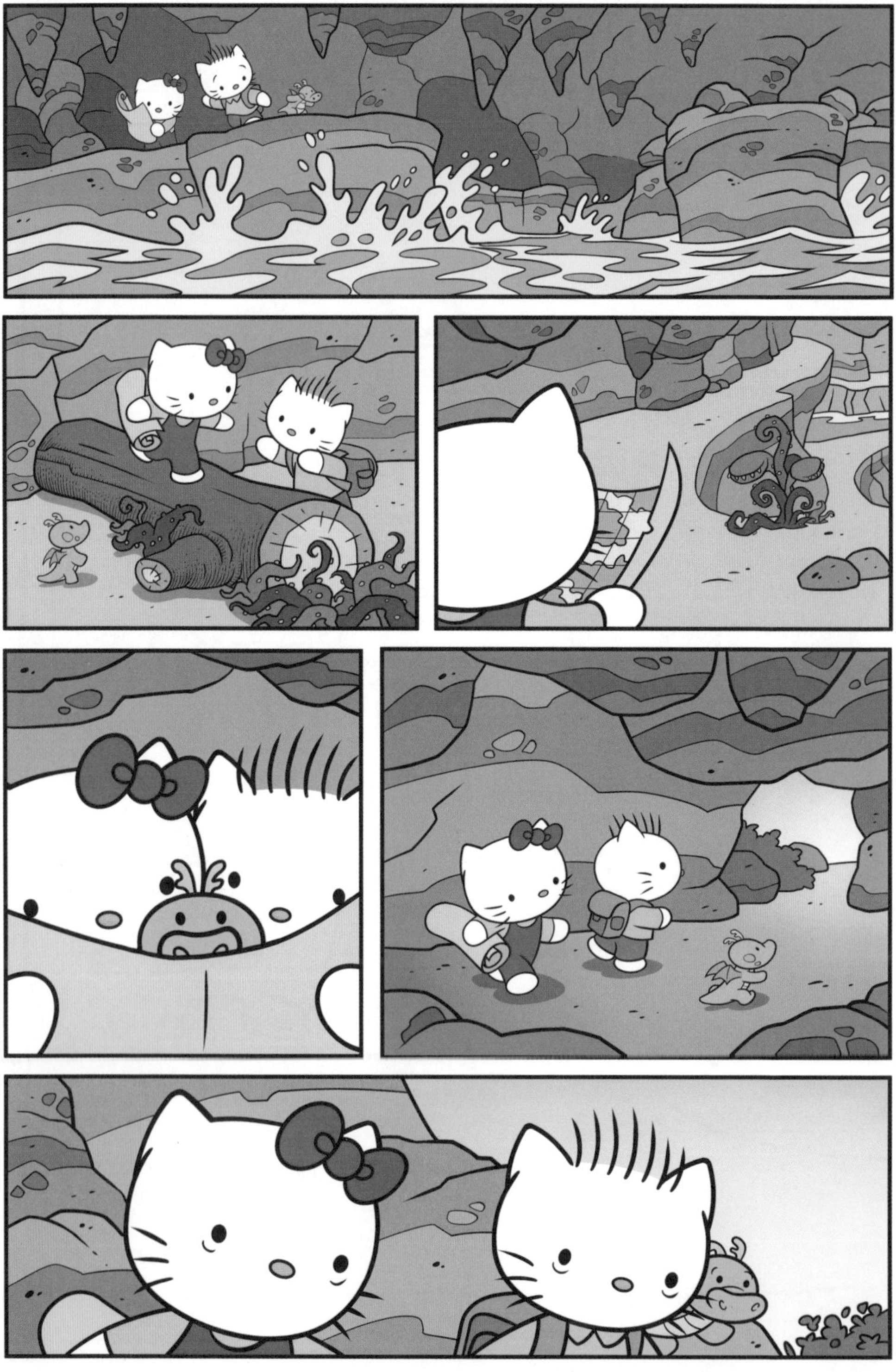

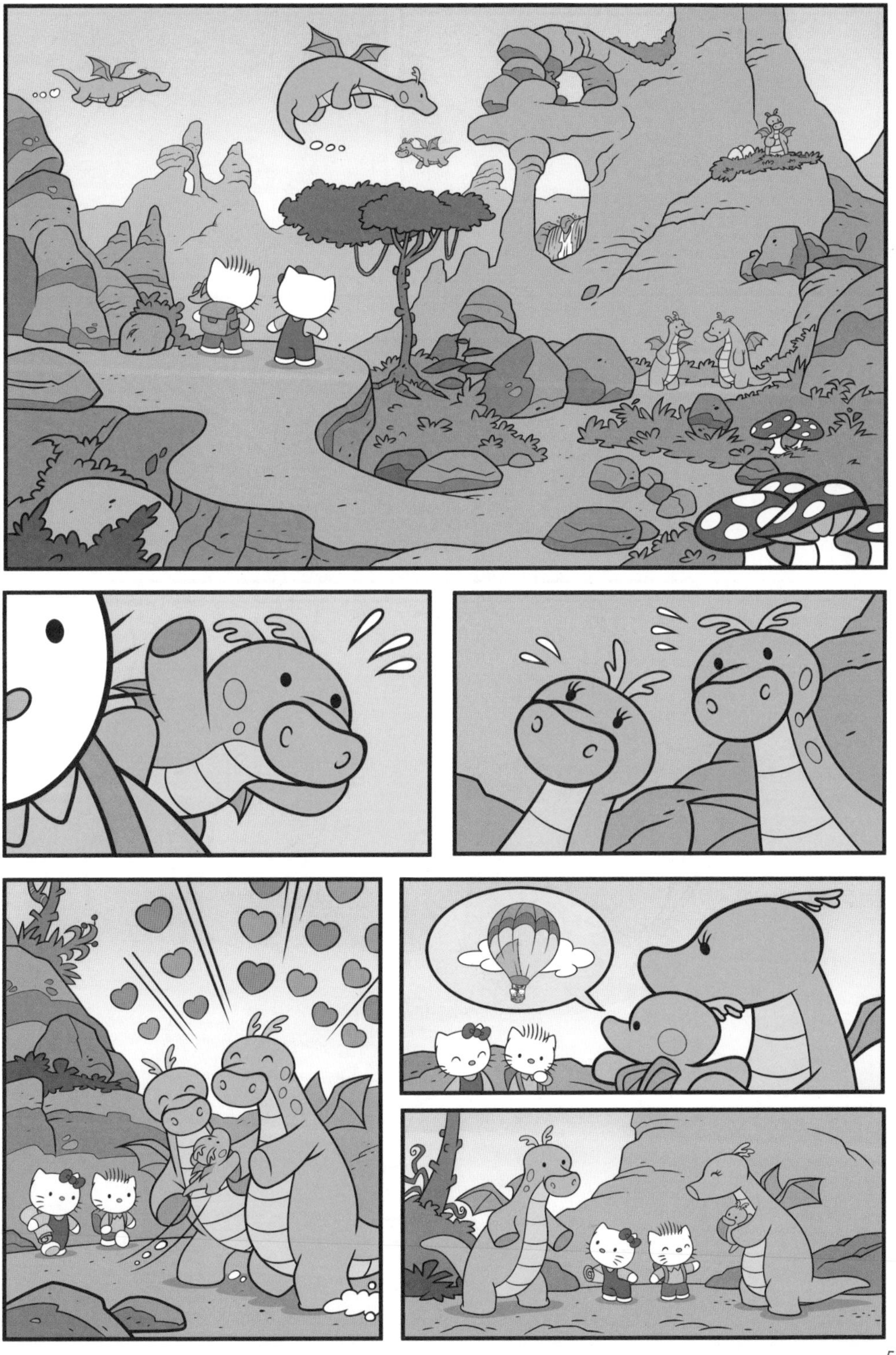

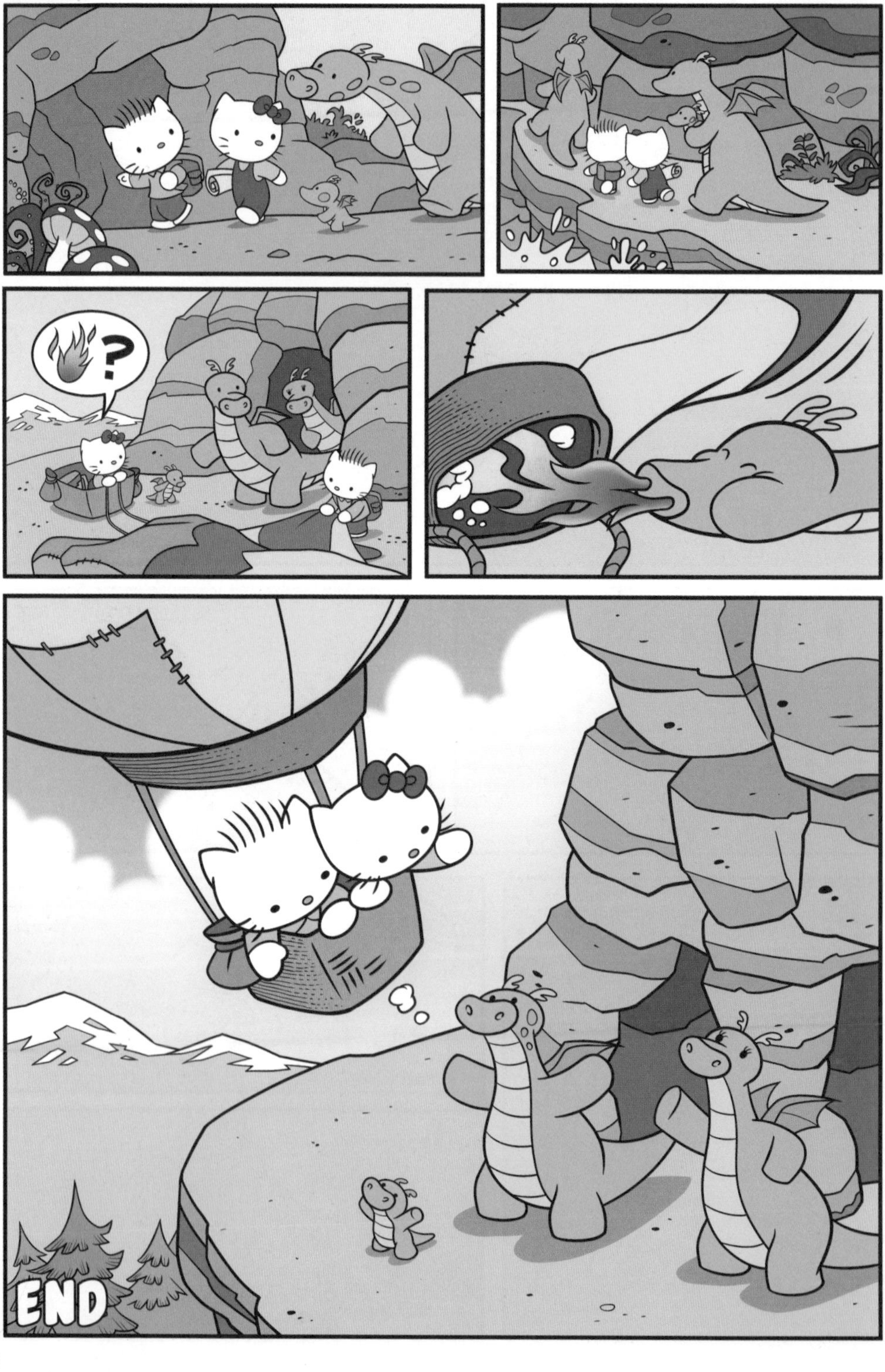
?
END

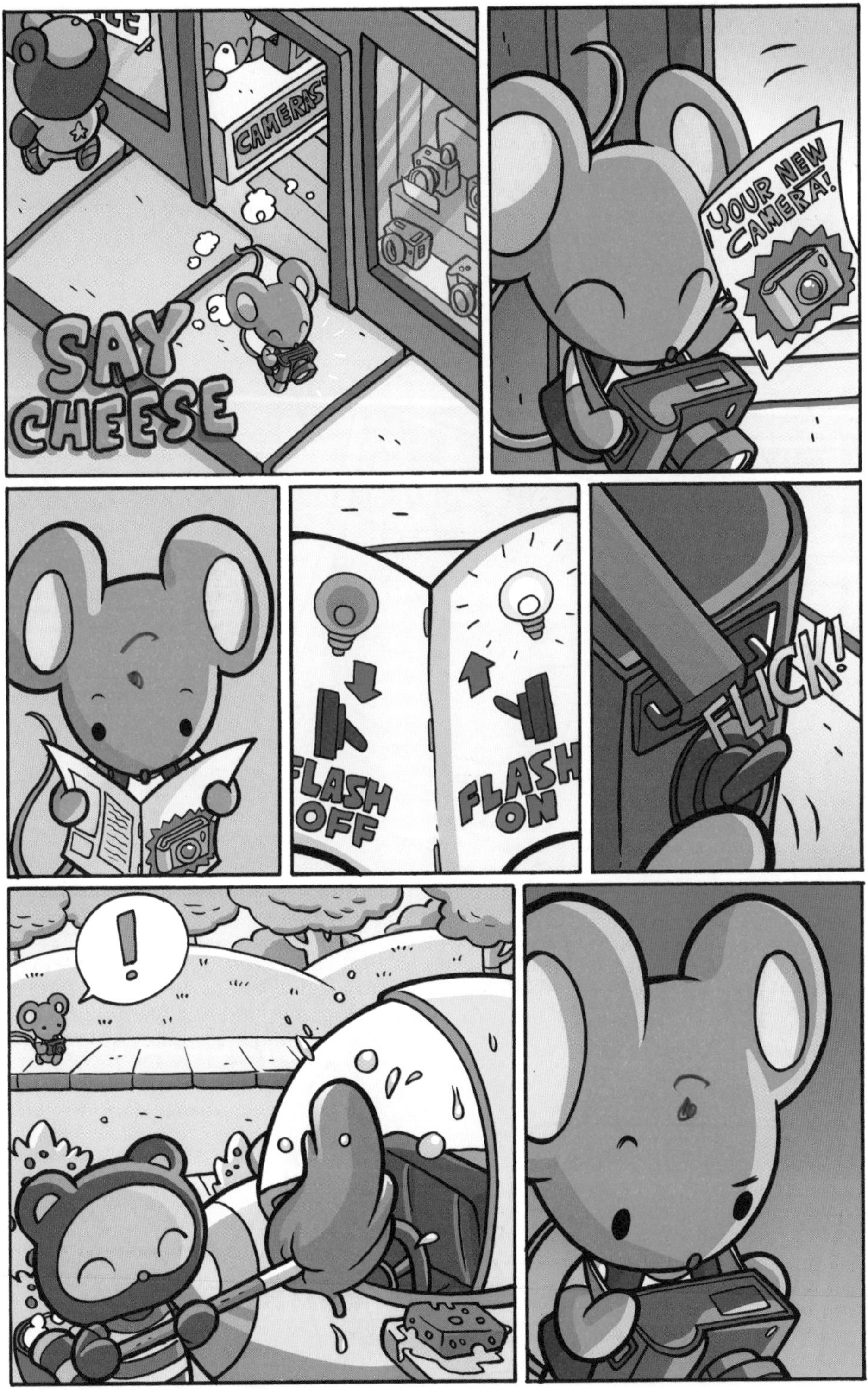
CAMERAS
SAY CHEESE
YOUR NEW CAMERA!
FLASH OFF
FLASH ON
FLICK!
!

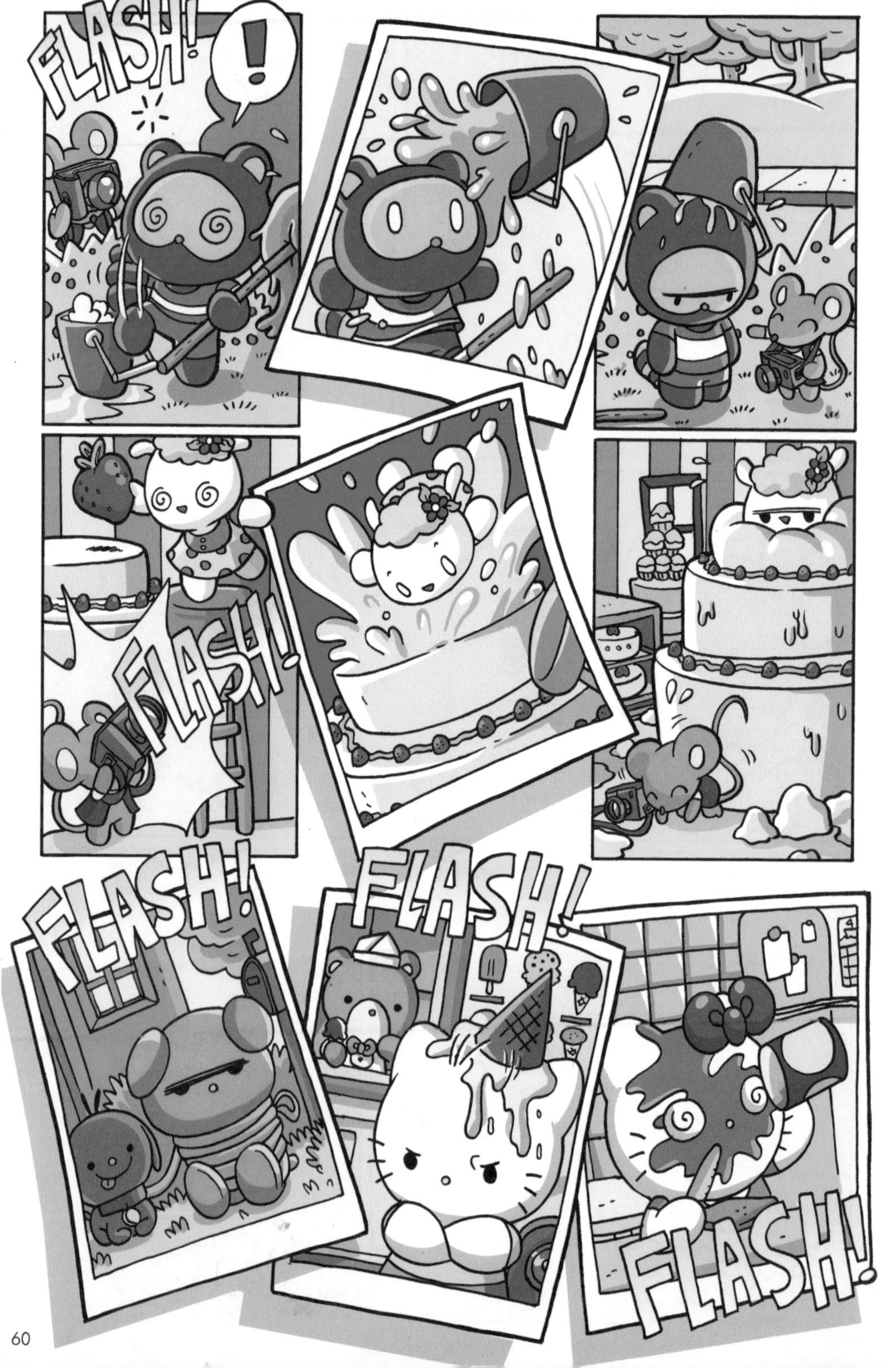
FLASH!
!
FLASH!
FLASH!
FLASH!
FLASH!

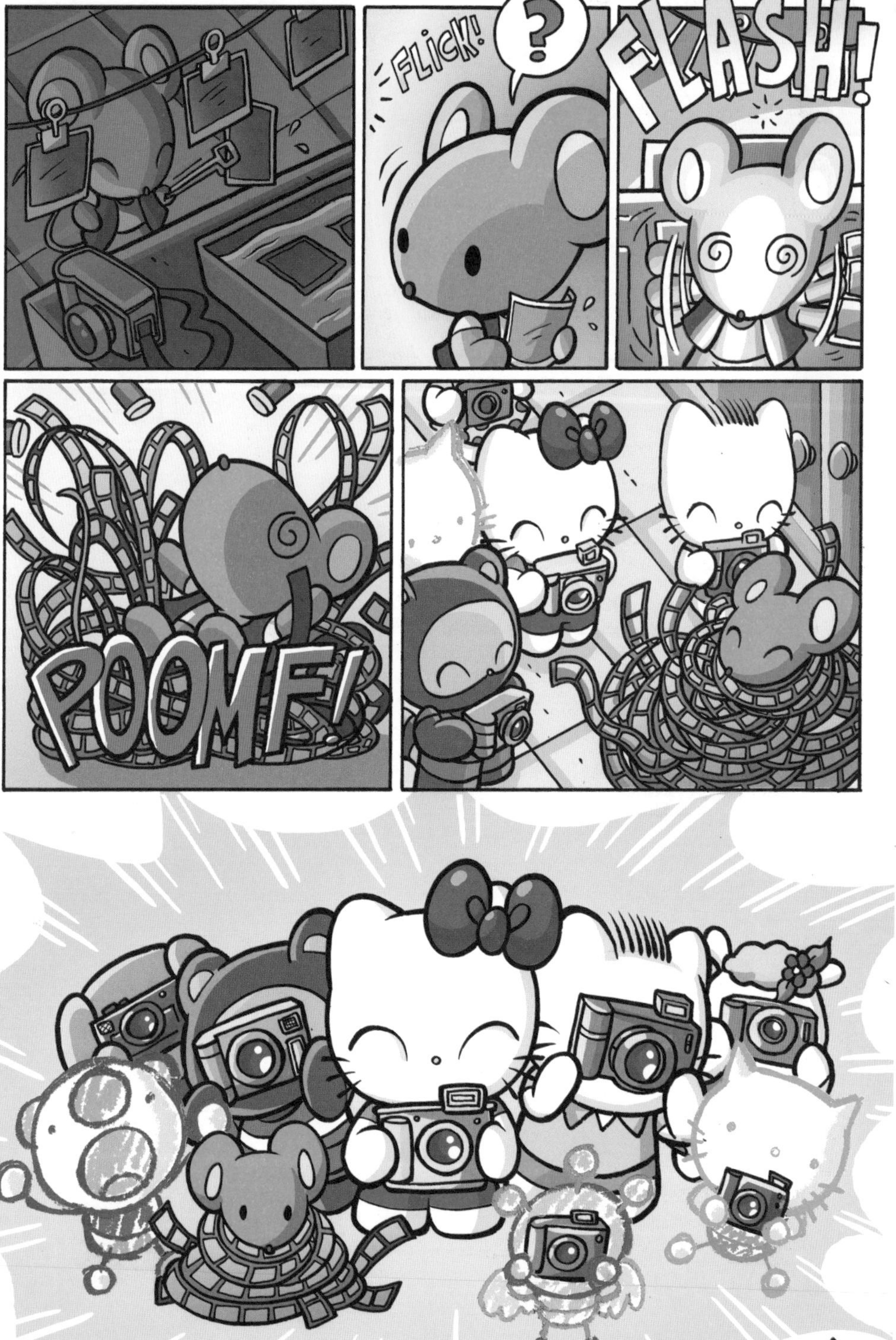
FLICK!
?
FLASH!
POOMF!
END!

Creators

Giovanni Castro was born in Colombia, studied art there, and now lives and works in Barcelona, Spain. He works mainly in editorial illustration and comics, which he loves a lot. He used to work with traditional media, but nowadays he does his illustrations digitally. He loves science fiction and historical themes and is interested in history, art and languages.

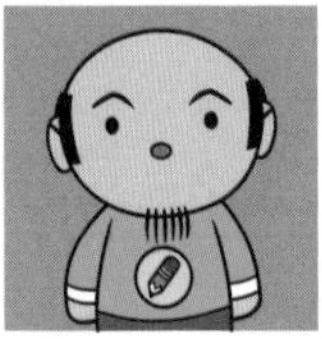

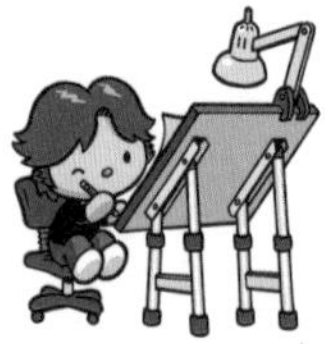

Jacob Chabot is a New York City-based cartoonist and illustrator. His comics have appeared in publications such as *Nickelodeon Magazine*, *Mad Magazine*, *Spongebob Comics*, and various Marvel titles. He also illustrated *Voltron Force: Shelter from the Storm* and *Voltron Force: True Colors* for VIZ Media. His comic *The Mighty Skullboy Army* is published through Dark Horse and in 2008 was nominated for an Eisner Award for Best Book for Teens.

Jorge Monlongo makes comic books, editorial and children's illustrations and video game designs and paints on canvas and walls. He combines traditional and digital techniques to create worlds in beautiful colors that usually hide terrible secrets. You can see his works in the press (*El Pais*, *Muy interesante*, *Rolling Stone*) and read his comic book series, *Mameshiba*, published by VIZ Media in the USA.

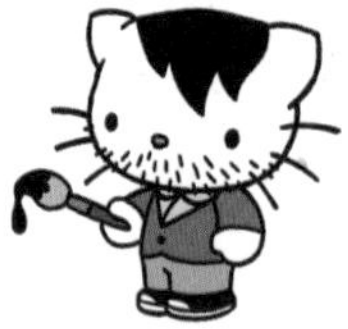

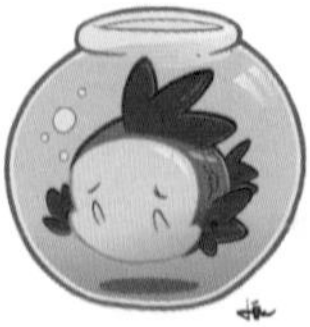

Ian McGinty lives in Savannah, Georgia, and also parts of the universe! Also, Earth. When he isn't drawing comics and rad pictures of octopuses (octopi?), he's laughing at funny-looking dogs and making low-carb burritos! Ian draws stuff for VIZ Media, Top Shelf Productions, BOOM! Studios, Zenescope and many more cool folk! But he cannot draw garbage trucks for some reason.

Maite Oz is an Argentinian illustrator based in Sweden who works on projects ranging from textile design to editorial illustrations. She loves nature, plants and stories with drawings. ♥

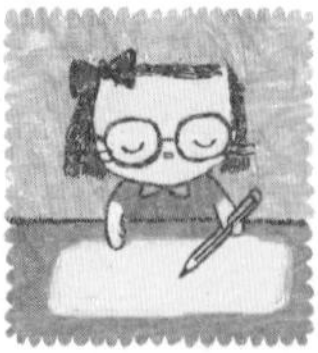

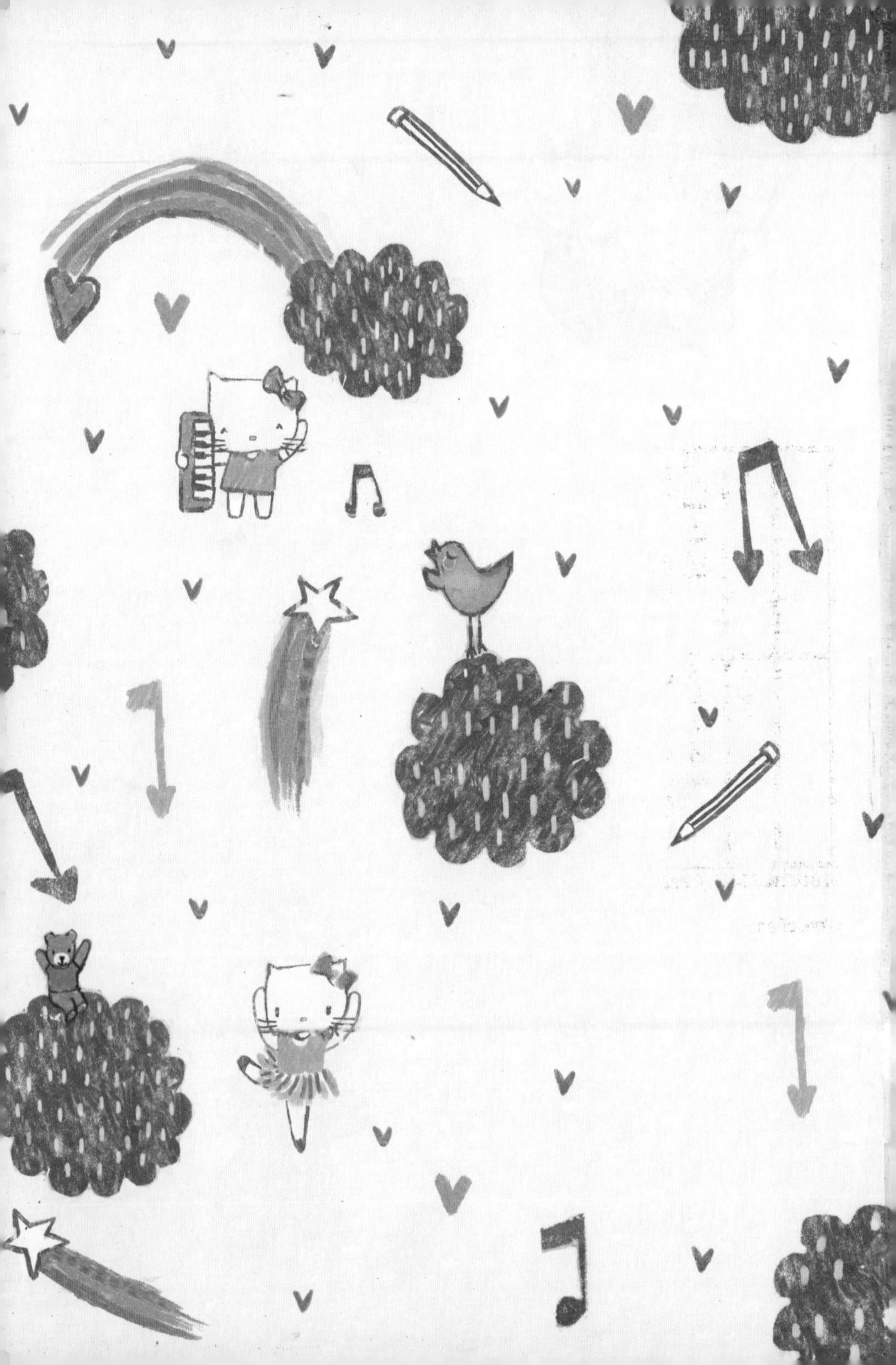